NIGHT
in the
FRONT LINE

edited and introduced by
ANN-MARIE EINHAUS

First published 2017 by
The British Library
96 Euston Road
London NW1 2DB

Cataloguing in Publication Data
A catalogue record for this book is available from the British Library

ISBN 978 0 7123 5697 8

Introduction and notes copyright © 2017 Ann-Marie Einhaus

Cover by Rawshock Design
Typeset by Tetragon, London
Printed in England by TJ International

CONTENTS

Looking Ahead

INTRODUCTION

In 1945, reflecting on the experience of war on the home front, novelist and short story writer Elizabeth Bowen observed:

> People whose homes had been blown up went to infinite lengths to assemble bits of themselves—broken ornaments, odd shoes, torn scraps of the curtains that had hung in a room—from the wreckage. In the same way, they assembled and checked themselves from stories and poems, from their memories, from one another's talk.[1]

Like its predecessor, the Second World War sparked the writing and publication of hundreds of short stories: in the words of writer and anthologist Dan Davin, in the Second World War, 'as in the Great War, writing somehow got done' despite the dangers and distractions, perhaps because there was a deep psychological need for storytelling.[2] While many of these short stories were written by and for civilian readers, stories were also read and written by servicemen and women, including Davin. They appeared in magazines and collections during and after the war, and addressed all areas of the conflict, from the home front to service abroad. Short stories offer a wonderful insight into everyday concerns on the various frontlines and illustrate the humour that kept up morale as well as the despair and confusion felt by so many. Some authors who captured the experience of the Second World War in short fiction are still very well known today, particularly those who also published longer novels: Elizabeth Bowen, Graham Greene and Christopher Isherwood are household names of modern British fiction. But given how central a place the Second World War holds in Britain's national memory, there are surprisingly few anthologies dedicated specifically to short stories about the war, and fewer are still readily available in print. This anthology hopes to introduce interested readers to a small selection of stories that are both unique representations of individual war experience and representative of larger trends.

Two anthologies collect the largest number of Second World War stories between them, some of which are included here: Dan Davin's *Short Stories from the Second World War* (1982) and Anne Boston's *Wave Me Goodbye: Stories of the Second World War* (1988). These two volumes cover two rather different sides of the conflict. Davin—himself a veteran as well as a short story writer—chose to focus primarily on the combatant experience of the war, although he strove to cover 'as many aspects as possible of the British at war in the years 1939 to 1945' and was impatient with fellow editors who dismissed home front stories as irrelevant.[3] Despite his understanding of the importance of the home front, it is perhaps not surprising that a veteran would be drawn particularly to depictions of combat in its various forms. Anne Boston's anthology remedies this bias by looking particularly at women's experiences of the Second World War. As her title suggests, these often involved painfully remaining behind as loved ones went to fight, but her selection shows that women were by no means only passive sufferers in the war. Besides Davin's and Boston's collections, most Second World War anthologies rely largely on extracts from longer prose texts alongside letters and poetry, including Ronald Blythe's *The Components of the Scene: An Anthology of the Prose and Poetry of the Second World War* (1966), which was reprinted several times, and Robert Hewison's home front collection *Under Siege: Literary Life in London 1939–1945* (1977).

Even more so than the First World War, the Second encouraged writers to turn to the short story for its brevity, as its shortness seemed to lend itself to the portrayal of lives and communities fragmented by war. The impact of the Blitz and the effect of rationing and all-out mobilization meant that it was not only combatants whose lives were constantly liable to interruption, often both sudden and deadly, as we can see from Bowen's comment cited at the start of this introduction. A short story or sketch could convey the confused impressions, the incidents witnessed without a chance to find out how they ended, the fleeting acquaintances made in air-raid shelters, better than longer prose. Practical reasons also played a part, however. In June 1940, Cyril Connolly reflected on the importance of brevity in the sixth issue of his new literary magazine, *Horizon*, daringly founded in times of frequent disruptions to paper supplies. He argued that '[it] is a secret of good writing that it takes up very little room and expands in the remembering', and took an optimistic approach to the effect of the wartime paper shortage.[4] The shortage, Connolly claimed, would merely rid the country 'of the books not worth publishing and the news not worth printing', and, he hoped, would strengthen the appeal of poetry, 'the only kind of writing so concentrated as to be economically justified' in times of war.[5] Next to poetry, however, Connolly championed equally 'economical' forms such as 'the short story, the critical essay, and, where we can find it, the imaginative writing which was once known as the prose poem'.[6] It was perhaps because the short story combined an economy of resources with an economy and flexibility of form that (in Davin's words) it 'proved to be one of the hardiest blooms to survive in a time of devastation and weeds'.[7]

This collection approaches stories about the Second World War from two angles: time and occupation. The first section, 'Looking Back', includes stories that explore the relationship between the Second World War and its predecessor, as the advent of the next war prompts these stories' protagonists to look back at the last one. The two middle sections are divided between stories offering us an insight into civilian life at home and service both at home and abroad. 'Looking Ahead'—the final section—concludes the volume with two stories situated at the end of the war, which encourage reflection on how one might move on from the experience of war.

Looking back

It was perhaps natural for writers during the Second World War, especially in its early stages, to refer to their most recent experience of another war, and references to the First World War in fiction about the Second abound.[8] These references often take the shape of throw-away comments and comparisons, as in Mollie Panter-Downes's 'Meeting at the Pringles''. Her village ladies, intent on aiding the war effort, can look back on their war work in the previous war, which serves as a source of expertise and authority. Having lost her own father at Mons at the outset of the First World War, when she was not yet ten years old, it is perhaps not surprising that Panter-Downes herself would think back to the First World War in the face of the Second. Similarly, fictional Mrs Miniver in Jan Struther's 'Gas Masks' lived through the First World War as a young girl, and cannot help but compare her experience of mingled ignorance and prejudice in the last war with what she sees as the greater maturity, the more balanced outlook of young people in the new war just starting. Looking back to the previous war could also become a more substantial part of a story's plot beyond throwaway reminiscences. Victoria Stewart has said of Bowen's inter-war stories that they had 'only an oblique relationship to the supernatural, concerning themselves not explicitly with *revenants*, but with what Bowen terms "the horror latent behind reality"'.[9] 'The Demon Lover', read symbolically as well as literally, concerns itself with both: the fearful return of the fiancé believed killed in the First World War, and the realization of the horror of war that lurks behind the seemingly calm façade of carrying on in the face of everyday violence.

Civilians and war workers

The Home Front of the Second World War, and particularly the experience of the Blitz, has become a crucial part of British popular memory and national identity. Most younger Britons will associate it with tales of unprecedented bravery and solidarity across class boundaries, and with nostalgic merchandise of the 'Keep Calm and Carry On' variety. However, the stories chosen for this volume complicate the picture by showing us not only the brave face and the stiff upper lip, but also the bewilderment and the at times selfish terror experienced by those affected, as in Molly Lefebure's 'Night in the Front Line'. Fred Urquhart's and William Sansom's stories offer us two rather different takes on those who took up war-related occupations during the war. Urquhart's land girls, working on farms to serve the needs of a nation at war, encounter the temporary hardships they face in high spirits. They seem aware of the uniqueness of their experience, and are confident that their wartime lives will at the very least make for a good story in years to come. Sansom's volunteer firemen, on the other hand, are very much caught up in the terrifying yet surreal moment. They serve as a reminder that frontline service, so to speak, did not necessarily involve going abroad.

Combatants

The stories in this section look at different kinds of experience of active service during the Second World War. Julian Maclaren-Ross's 'I had to go sick' gives us insight into the equally comical and frustrating experience of the civilian-turned-soldier. His narrator finds himself trapped in a bizarre tussle with circuitous army regulations before he is even posted abroad. By contrast, the next two stories—Alun Lewis's 'The Orange Grove' and Roald Dahl's 'A Piece of Cake'—do take us abroad to Burma and North Africa respectively. H. E. Bates's 'The Disinherited', written as part of a Royal Air Force publicity drive to promote the crucial work undertaken by RAF pilots and ground staff, also puts the British war effort in touch with the wider world. Bates's story centres on Capek, a Czech fighter pilot who has managed to escape from Nazi-occupied Europe and is now flying night missions for the RAF. The picture Bates paints of the RAF is of an organization in which men (and women) 'from all over the world' are united in their fight against Nazism: Dutch and Polish, Belgian and Czech, French and Norwegian, Swiss and American, as well as British and French colonial troops from the Far East, Africa and the Caribbean, Canada, Australia and New Zealand.[10] His story showed readers then as much as it reminds us today that victory over fascism was owed to international bonds of friendship and collaboration.

Looking ahead

Elizabeth Taylor's 'Gravement Endommagé' is a curious case of simultaneously looking forwards and backwards. The French provincial city destroyed by the Second World War in which the protagonist and his wife find themselves on their way to Paris recalls to the husband similar devastation he witnessed during the First World War—and this recollection affects his ability to look ahead with vigour and optimism. Reconstruction seems under the shadow of a sense of *déjà vu* that suggests rebuilding is futile: not only with regards to physical reconstruction, but also with regards to the rebuilding of relationships that have cracked under the strain of war. The difficulty of moving on is also emphasized in Inez Holden's 'According to the Directive'. The setting of this story is a camp for Displaced Persons on the Continent, where the protagonist encounters those whom war has left in limbo: their old lives have been destroyed by war, in many cases alongside their entire families, but their future is as yet uncertain.

I feel that the stories collected in this anthology serve to challenge Davin's notion that the majority of short stories published during the war 'faded like the cheap paper of the little magazines in which they were printed, or like the photographs in old wartime albums, meaningful only to those who shared the experience they recall and incapable of transmitting it to those who did not.'[11] It is my firm belief that these stories illustrate unique human experiences that can still speak to us today, and I hope that you enjoy reading all of them, whether they are by well-known authors or writers forgotten today.

ANN-MARIE EINHAUS

NOTES

1 Elizabeth Bowen, *The Mulberry Tree: Writings of Elizabeth Bowen*, ed. by Hermione Lee (London: Virago, 1986), p. 97.

2 Dan Davin, 'Introduction', in *Short Stories from the Second World War* (Oxford: Oxford University Press, 1982), pp. i–xiv (p. xiv).

3 Davin, 'Introduction', pp. i, x.

4 Cyril Connolly, editor's comment in *Horizon* 1.6 (June 1940), p. 392.

5 Ibid.

6 Ibid.

7 Davin, 'Introduction', p. ix.

8 See for example Victoria Stewart, 'The Last War: The Legacy of the First World War in 1940s British Fiction', in *British Popular Culture and the First World War*, ed. by Jessica Meyer (Leiden: Brill, 2008), pp. 259–81.

9 Victoria Stewart, 'Violence and Representation in Elizabeth Bowen's Interwar Short Stories', *English*, 58.221 (2009), pp. 139–59 (pp. 139–40).

10 H. E. Bates, 'The Disinherited', in *Short Stories from the Second World War*, ed. Dan Davin, pp. 89–92 (p. 89).

11 Davin, 'Introduction', p. xiv.

Looking Back

MEETING AT THE PRINGLES'

Mollie Panter-Downes (1906–1997)

Panter-Downes was a novelist and journalist who wrote her first novel, *The Shoreless Sea* (1923), as a teenager. She was a regular contributor to the *New Yorker* for most of her adult life, and for the duration of the Second World War supplied a regular column entitled 'Letters from London', which gave American readers an insight into life in wartime Britain. Panter-Downes's wartime short stories also all appeared in the *New Yorker*, and like her non-fiction, chronicle the lives and experiences of ordinary British people at war: rationing, leave-taking, evacuees and war work all feature in her snapshots of home front life. 'Meeting at the Pringles'' draws clear comparisons between the Second World War and its predecessor, as Panter-Downes's village ladies fall back on their memories of war work undertaken in the last war.

T HE COMMITTEE MET IN THE DRAWING-ROOM AT Laburnum Cottage, the home of two ladies invariably known as the Pringle girls. One of the Pringle girls had been wedded and widowed and was now Mrs Carver. Neither of them was likely to see fifty again, but Pringle girls they remained, their girlishness rather ghoulishly preserved, like the dried flowers and pampas grass that rustled in the draught from the drawing-room door. The room was extremely cold. Although it was a chilly evening, there was no fire in the grate, nothing but a pyramid of more dried vegetable matter—pine cones this time, gilded and backed by a fan of pleated pink paper. It occurred to Mrs Taylor that the committee would be a good deal cosier in the dining-room, where she had noticed the stout terrier Chappie wheezing on the rug in front of a bright little fire. Tradition, however, demanded that committees should meet in the drawing-room. Mrs Taylor sighed, crossed her stout legs in their grey woollen stockings, and gazed expectantly at Mrs Peake, who had risen to address the meeting.

Mrs Peake explained that the committee had been called together to organize a Hospital Supplies Depot in the village.

She was opening proceedings in her capacity as chairman of the local Women's Voluntary Services because *someone* had to do it—otherwise there was no reason Miss Craddock, representing the Personal Service League, or Mrs Taylor, secretary of the Women's Institute, should not be in the chair.

'Nonsense, Doris, you do it much better,' said Miss Craddock briskly.

Mrs Peake said she just wanted to make it clear that there were going to be no particular bosses on this job and that all the different village interests were going to pool their resources for the one cause. She would now call on Mrs Carver to tell them more about the scheme, and, before sitting down, she would like to propose that Mrs Carver, who had done such excellent work in the Great War, should be elected as officer-in-charge of the whole organization.

'I second that,' snapped Miss Craddock.

Mrs Carver said unconvincingly that it was very nice of everybody, but she didn't know why it should be her. The committee murmured polite encouragement.

'Well, if I could have Lois to help me,' Mrs Carver said, 'I mean it's going to be quite a big job. It will take two of us easily.'

The unmarried Pringle girl, folding her arms across her thin bosom, stared gloomily at her sister through her pince-nez. 'I don't know whether I'd be much help,' she said. 'I never did have any brains, you know that, Alice.'

'Then that's carried unanimously!' Mrs Peake cried. 'Mrs Carver has kindly promised to be our officer-in-charge, with

Miss Lois Pringle as her second-in-command. Although this is such an informal meeting, I think someone ought to take a few notes, don't you?'

The election was duly recorded by Mrs Taylor, and the ladies gave their attention to Mrs Carver.

'Before we go any further, we've got to decide what work we're going to do and where we're going to do it,' Mrs Carver announced. 'I've been to see one or two people about it already. Lois and I drove in to Sherbury this morning to see Mrs Peters, the Regional Organizer, and I must say that what she had to say was rather upsetting. In the first place, if we want to make any surgical dressings at all, we must supply a room which can be passed as completely sterile by the medical authorities. Walls and floor washed down every time it's been used, you know, and all that nonsense. "If you insist on a room like that," I said to Mrs Peters, "you won't get a single splint made in any village the length and breadth of England." I said to her, "In the last war my sister and I made surgical swabs by the thousand just in Mrs Robertson's drawing-room—and there wasn't anything particularly sterile about *that*." "Well," said Mrs Peters, "I quite see your point, Mrs Carver, and I can't say that I'm not in sympathy with you, but those at the minute are the orders from headquarters."'

A babble of dismayed talk broke out. Everyone agreed that it was ridiculous and that there wasn't a room to meet those requirements in the village.

'How about the stage at the Village Hall?' suggested Mrs Taylor. 'It's nice and bare, and I suppose we could get it scrubbed after we used it.'

'My dear, *think* of the germs in those curtains,' said Mrs Peake, shuddering. 'All the children acting scenes from *As You Like It* and simply septic with colds and chicken pox. I really don't think it would be awfully good. How about the big play-room at the Dysons'?'

Miss Craddock reminded her that the Dysons were sleeping twenty mothers and children evacuated from London.

'There's the room at The George,' said Miss Pringle doubtfully.

'Good gracious, Lois! You don't want the dressings to reek of beer, do you?' Miss Craddock said.

'Well, if it's quite agreed that we are unable to produce a pure room in this village,' Mrs Peake said playfully, 'I should like to say that Miss Judd has kindly offered her drawing-room and study for the use of the working party. It's got a lot to recommend it. It's central—'

'That's another thing,' said Mrs Taylor. 'Now that we haven't got the petrol, you've got to think how people are going to get in to the Depot.'

Mrs Peake said that they would have to consider the practicality of having one central Depot and one or two lesser ones in different parts of the village. Lady Buxton had rung her up yesterday and asked if they would like her to start a small working party at Croom, just for tenants' wives and people around. Mrs Peake had explained that of course such a party would have to be affiliated as an offshoot of Mrs Carver's, and that if Mrs Carver had no objection—

'Not in the least,' said Mrs Carver. 'Let her have an offshoot by all means. Let's hear more about Miss Judd's drawing-room. I can't remember if it's got cupboards or not. In the last war we used to put the work away in cardboard boxes, but in this war I suppose we'll have to be a good deal more fussy.'

After some discussion, Mrs Taylor was able to record a resolution that it was decided to accept Miss Judd's kind offer of rooms for the working party.

'I think we'll have to start a little subscription for lighting and heating,' said Mrs Peake.

'Yes, we'll have to have some sort of heating,' agreed Mrs Carver.

The committee politely hid their lavender knuckles and agreed.

'It's wonderful, though, how the dahlias kept on,' said Mrs Taylor. 'They were a sight this year. Our Jane Cowls are really a picture, only we find them a little difficult to keep from year to year—I don't know why.'

Mrs Taylor was led back sternly from tubers to pneumonia jackets by Mrs Carver, who said that she would write up to the Red Cross for patterns. At first, she supposed, they had better concentrate on such surgical supplies as they would be allowed to make in the septic surroundings of Miss Judd's drawing-room. She put her glasses in their case and snapped it shut, as though the Regional Organizer's neck were inside it.

Mrs Peake, gathering the meeting together with a smiling glance, said, 'If no other lady has any more questions to ask, I almost think we might adjourn.'

No other lady had. The committee started getting to their feet and inserting their lifeless hands into doeskin gloves. The Pringle girls came to the front door and waved goodbye, first to Miss Craddock, who got on her bicycle and shot off into the twilight, then to Mrs Peake and Mrs Taylor, who were going in Mrs Peake's car. At the bow window in the dining-room, the figure of the Pringles' little maid could be seen, mounted on a carved Ashanti stool and struggling wildly among the folds of black rep with which she was completing the Laburnum Cottage blackout.

'Then I'll ring up Lady Buxton tonight about her offshoot!' shouted Mrs Carver.

'Do!' cried Mrs Peake. 'I know she'll be helpful.'

The ladies drove away and the Pringle girls went indoors to sit by the dining-room fire with Chappie and the wireless. They had missed the six o'clock news, but at nine o'clock the familiar gentlemanly voice told bits about the war and the King and ration cards. After it was over, Mrs Carver went out into the hall to telephone Lady Buxton. Lois could hear her voice, brisk and cheerful, in the pauses between 'Tipperary' and other jolly old favourites that the B.B.C. was relaying from a soldiers' concert party.

'It's a long way to Tipperar-ee—'

'Of course it's nonsense!' Mrs Carver was shouting into the telephone. 'I said to Mrs Peters that you'd never find a perfectly antiseptic room in any village. "In the last war," I said to her—'

'But my heart's right there!' roared the voices of the potential customers in whose service the ladies were being so busy and happy—happier, as a matter of fact, than they had been for the last twenty-one years.

GAS MASKS

Jan Struther [Joyce Anstruther] (1901–1953)

Struther—born as Joyce Anstruther and later married as Joyce
Maxtone Graham and Joyce Placzek respectively—published
several collections of poems, a book of children's verse, *The
Modern Struwwelpeter* (1936), and a collection of stories, *Mrs
Miniver* (1939). She is also known for writing a number of
hymns. Before it was included in *Mrs Miniver*, 'Gas Masks' first
appeared as part of a regular column in *The Times* which had
commenced in 1937, and Mrs Miniver, her family and friends
were an international wartime success, particularly in the U.S.,
where readers were keen to get a glimpse of life under siege
in the U.K. Struther in fact moved to the U.S. with her family
to work as a lecturer early on in the war.

CLEM HAD TO GO AND GET HIS MASK EARLY, ON HIS WAY to the office, but the rest of them went at half past one, hoping that the lunch hour would be less crowded. It may have been: but even so there was a longish queue. They were quite a large party—Mrs Miniver and Nannie; Judy and Toby; Mrs Adie, the Scots cook, lean as a winter aspen, and Gladys, the new house-parlourmaid: a pretty girl, with complicated hair. Six of them—or seven if you counted Toby's Teddy bear, which seldom left his side, and certainly not if there were any treats about. For to children, even more than to grown-ups (and this is at once a consolation and a danger), any excitement really counts as a treat, even if it is a painful excitement like breaking your arm, or a horrible excitement like seeing a car smash, or a terrifying excitement like playing hide-and-seek in the shrubbery at dusk. Mrs Miniver herself had been nearly grown-up in August 1914, but she remembered vividly how her younger sister had exclaimed with shining eyes, 'I say! I'm in a war!'

But she clung to the belief that this time, at any rate, children of Vin's and Judy's age had been told beforehand what it was all about, had heard both sides, and had discussed it themselves with a touching and astonishing maturity. If the worst came to the worst (it was funny how one still shied away from saying, 'If there's a war', and fell back on euphemisms)— if the worst came to the worst, these children would at least know that we were fighting against an idea, and not against a nation. Whereas the last generation had been told to run and play in the garden, had been shut out from the grown-ups' worried conclaves: and then quite suddenly had all been plunged into an orgy of licensed lunacy, of boycotting Grimm and Struwwelpeter, of looking askance at their cousins' old Fraulein, and of feeling towards Dachshund puppies the uneasy tenderness of a devout churchwoman dandling her daughter's love-child. But this time those lunacies—or rather, the outlook which bred them—must not be allowed to come into being. To guard against that was the most important of all the forms of war work which she and other women would have to do: there are no tangible gas masks to defend us in wartime against its slow, yellow, drifting corruption of the mind.

The queue wormed itself on a little. They moved out of the bright, noisy street into the sunless corridors of the Town Hall. But at least there were benches to sit on. Judy produced pencils and paper (she was a far-sighted child) and began play-ing Consequences with Toby. By the time they edged up to the end of the corridor Mr Chamberlain had met Shirley Temple in a Tube lift and Herr Hitler was closeted with Minnie Mouse in an even smaller rendezvous.

When they got into the Town Hall itself they stopped play-ing. Less than half an hour later they came out again into the sunlit street: but Mrs Miniver felt afterwards that during that half-hour she had said goodbye to something. To the last shreds which lingered in her, perhaps, of the old, false, traditional con-ception of glory. She carried away with her, as well as a litter of black rubber pigs, a series of detached impressions, like shots in a quick-cut film. Her own right hand with a pen in it, filling up six yellow cards in pleasurable block capitals; Mrs Adie sitting up as straight as a ramrod under the fitter's hands, betraying no signs of the apprehension which Mrs Miniver knew she must be feeling about her false fringe; Gladys's rueful giggle as her elaborate coiffure came out partially wrecked from her ordeal; the look of sudden realization in Judy's eyes just before her face was covered up; the back of Toby's neck, the valley deeper than usual because his muscles were taut with distaste (he had a horror of rubber in any form); a very small child bursting into a wail of dismay on catching sight of its mother disguised in a black snout; the mother's muffled reassurances—'It's on'y Mum, duck. Look—it's just a mask, like at Guy Fawkes, see?' (*Mea mater mala sus est*. Absurdly, she remembered the Latin catch Vin had told her, which can mean either 'My mother is a bad pig' or 'Run, mother, the pig is eating the apples.')

Finally, in another room, there were the masks themselves, stacked close, covering the floor like a growth of black fungus. They took what had been ordered for them—four medium size, two small—and filed out into the street.

It was for this, thought Mrs Miniver as they walked towards the car, that one had boiled the milk for their bottles, and washed their hands before lunch, and not let them eat with a spoon which had been dropped on the floor.

Toby said suddenly, with a chuckle, 'We ought to have got one for Teddy.' It would have been almost more bearable if he had said it seriously. But just as they were getting into the car a fat woman went past, with a fatter husband.

'You did look a fright,' she said. 'I 'ad to laugh.'

One had to laugh.

THE DEMON LOVER

Elizabeth Bowen (1899–1973)

Bowen was born into a wealthy Anglo-Irish family at the turn of the twentieth century.

'The Demon Lover' is one of Bowen's better-known stories, reprinted in *The Demon Lover and Other Stories* (1945) and *Ivy Gripped the Steps and Other Stories* (1946), and anthologized repeatedly since then. Bowen was fifteen when the First World War started, and although she did not lose any immediate family to the war, it was a melancholy time for her following the death of her mother a few years earlier, as she was brought up by relatives and moved between homes. Bowen's recollection of this time and its death toll almost certainly inform her story.

TOWARDS THE END OF HER DAY IN LONDON MRS DROVER went round to her shut-up house to look for several things she wanted to take away. Some belonged to herself, some to her family, who were by now used to their country life. It was late August; it had been a steamy, showery day: at the moment the trees down the pavement glittered in an escape of humid yellow afternoon sun. Against the next batch of clouds, already piling up ink-dark, broken chimneys and parapets stood out. In her once familiar street, as in any unused channel, an unfamiliar queerness had silted up; a cat wove itself in and out of railings, but no human eye watched Mrs Drover's return. Shifting some parcels under her arm, she slowly forced round her latchkey in an unwilling lock, then gave the door, which had warped, a push with her knee. Dead air came out to meet her as she went in.

The staircase window having been boarded up, no light came down into the hall. But one door, she could just see, stood ajar, so she went quickly through into the room and unshuttered the big window in there. Now the prosaic woman, looking about her, was more perplexed than she knew by everything that she saw, by traces of her long former habit of life—the yellow smoke-stain up the white marble mantelpiece, the ring left by a vase on the top of the escritoire; the bruise in the wallpaper where, on the door being thrown open widely, the china handle had always hit the wall. The piano, having gone away to be stored, had left what looked like claw-marks on its part of the parquet. Though not much dust had seeped in, each object wore a film of another kind; and, the only ventilation being the chimney, the whole drawing-room smelled of the cold hearth. Mrs Drover put down her parcels on the escritoire and left the room to proceed upstairs; the things she wanted were in a bedroom chest.

She had been anxious to see how the house was—the part-time caretaker she shared with some neighbours was away this week on his holiday, known to be not yet back. At the best of times he did not look in often, and she was never sure that she trusted him. There were some cracks in the structure, left by the last bombing, on which she was anxious to keep an eye. Not that one could do anything—

A shaft of refracted daylight now lay across the hall. She stopped dead and stared at the hall table—on this lay a letter addressed to her.

She thought first—then the caretaker *must* be back. All the same, who, seeing the house shuttered, would have dropped a letter in at the box? It was not a circular, it was not a bill. And the post office redirected, to the address in the country, everything for her that came through the post. The caretaker (even if he *were* back) did not know she was due in London today—her call here had been planned to be a surprise—so his negligence in the manner of this letter, leaving it to wait in the dusk and the dust, annoyed her. Annoyed, she picked up the letter, which bore no stamp. But it cannot be important, or they would know... She took the letter rapidly upstairs with her, without a stop to look at the writing till she reached what had been her bedroom, where she let in light. The room looked over the garden and other gardens: the sun had gone in; as the clouds sharpened and lowered, the trees and rank lawns seemed already to smoke with dark. Her reluctance to look again at the letter came from the fact that she felt intruded upon—and by someone contemptuous of her ways. However, in the tenseness preceding the fall of rain she read it: it was a few lines.

Dear Kathleen,

You will not have forgotten that today is our anniversary, and the day we said. The years have gone by at once slowly and fast. In view of the fact that nothing has changed, I shall rely upon you to keep your promise. I was sorry to see you leave London, but was satisfied that you would be back in time. You may expect me, therefore, at the hour arranged.

Until then...

K.

Mrs Drover looked for the date: it was today's. She dropped the letter on to the bed-springs, then picked it up to see the writing again—her lips, beneath the remains of lipstick, beginning to go white. She felt so much the change in her own face that she went to the mirror, polished a clear patch in it and looked at once urgently and stealthily in. She was confronted by a woman of forty-four, with eyes starting out under a hat-brim that had been rather carelessly pulled down. She had not put on any more powder since she left the shop where she ate her solitary tea. The pearls her husband had given her on their marriage hung loose round her now rather thinner throat, slipping into the V of the pink wool jumper her sister knitted last autumn as they sat round the fire. Mrs Drover's most normal expression was one of controlled worry, but of assent. Since the birth of the third of her little boys, attended by a quite serious illness, she had had an intermittent muscular flicker to the left of her mouth, but in spite of this she could always sustain a manner that was at once energetic and calm.

Turning from her own face as precipitately as she had gone to meet it, she went to the chest where the things were, unlocked it, threw up the lid and knelt to search. But as rain began to come crashing down she could not keep from looking over her shoulder at the stripped bed on which the letter lay. Behind the blanket of rain the clock of the church that still stood struck six—with rapidly heightening apprehension she counted each of the slow strokes. 'The hour arranged... My God,' she said, '*what* hour? How should I...? After twenty-five years...'

The young girl talking to the soldier in the garden had not ever completely seen his face. It was dark; they were saying good-bye under a tree. Now and then—for it felt, from not seeing him at this intense moment, as though she had never seen him at all—she verified his presence for these few moments longer by putting out a hand, which he each time pressed, without very much kindness, and painfully, on to one of the breast buttons of his uniform. That cut of the button on the palm of her hand was, principally, what she was to carry away. This was so near the end of a leave from France that she could only wish him already gone. It was August 1916. Being not kissed, being drawn away from and looked at intimidated Kathleen till she imagined spectral glitters in the place of his eyes. Turning away and looking back up the lawn she saw, through branches of trees, the drawing-room window alight: she caught a breath for the moment when she could go running back there into the safe arms of her mother and sister, and cry: 'What shall I do, what shall I do? He has gone.'

Hearing her catch her breath, her fiancé said, without feeling: 'Cold?'

'You're going away such a long way.'

'Not so far as you think.'

'I don't understand?'

'You don't have to,' he said. 'You will. You know what we said.'

'But that was—suppose you—I mean, suppose.'

'I shall be with you,' he said, 'sooner or later. You won't forget that. You need do nothing but wait.'

Only a little more than a minute later she was free to run up the silent lawn. Looking in through the window at her mother and sister, who did not for the moment perceive her, she already felt that unnatural promise drive down between her and the rest of all human kind. No other way of having given herself could have made her feel so apart, lost and forlorn. She could not have plighted a more sinister troth.

Kathleen behaved well when, some months later, her fiancé was reported missing, presumed killed. Her family not only supported her but were able to praise her courage without stint because they could not regret, as a husband for her, the man they knew almost nothing about. They hoped she would, in a year or two, console herself—and had it been only a question of consolation things might have gone much straighter ahead. But her trouble, behind just a little grief, was a complete dislocation from everything. She did not reject other lovers, for these failed to appear: for years she failed to attract men—and with the approach of her 'thirties she became natural enough to share her family's anxiousness on this score. She began to put herself out, to wonder; and at thirty-two she was very greatly relieved to find herself being courted by William Drover. She married him, and the two of them settled down in this quiet, arboreal part of Kensington: in this house the years piled up, her children were born and they all lived till they were driven out by the bombs of the next war. Her movements as Mrs Drover were circumscribed, and she dismissed any idea that they were still watched.

As things were—dead or living the letter-writer sent her only a threat. Unable, for some minutes, to go on kneeling with her back exposed to the empty room, Mrs Drover rose from the chest to sit on an upright chair whose back was firmly against the wall. The desuetude of her former bedroom, her married London home's whole air of being a cracked cup from which memory, with its reassuring power, had either evaporated or leaked away, made a crisis—and at just this crisis the letter-writer had, knowledgeably, struck. The hollowness of the house this evening cancelled years on years of voices, habits and steps. Through the shut windows she only heard rain fall on the roofs around. To rally herself, she said she was in a mood—and, for two or three seconds shutting her eyes, told herself that she had imagined the letter. But she opened them—there it lay on the bed.

On the supernatural side of the letter's entrance she was not permitting her mind to dwell. Who, in London, knew she meant to call at the house today? Evidently, however,—this has been known. The caretaker, *had* he come back, had had no cause to expect her: he would have taken the letter in his pocket, to forward it, at his own time, through the post. There was no other sign that the caretaker had been in—but, if not? Letters dropped in at doors of deserted houses do not fly or walk to tables in halls. They do not sit on the dust of empty tables with the air of certainty that they will be found. There is needed some human hand—but nobody but the caretaker had a key. Under circumstances she did not care to consider, a house can be entered without a key. It was possible that she was not alone now. She might be being waited for, downstairs.

Waited for—until when? Until 'the hour arranged'. At least that was not six o'clock: six has struck.'

She rose from the chair and went over and locked the door.

The thing was, to get out. To fly? No, not that: she had to catch her train. As a woman whose utter dependability was the keystone of her family life she was not willing to return to the country, to her husband, her little boys and her sister, without the objects she had come up to fetch. Resuming work at the chest she set about making up a number of parcels in a rapid, fumbling-decisive way. These, with her shopping parcels, would be too much to carry; these meant a taxi—at the thought of the taxi her heart went up and her normal breathing resumed. I will ring up the taxi now; the taxi cannot come too soon: I shall hear the taxi out there running its engine, till I walk calmly down to it through the hall. I'll ring up—But no: the telephone is cut off... She tugged at a knot she had tied wrong.

The idea of flight... He was never kind to me, not really. I don't remember him kind at all. Mother said he never considered me. He was set on me, that was what it was—not love. Not love, not meaning a person well. What did he do, to make me promise like that? I can't remember—But she found that she could.

She remembered with such dreadful acuteness that the twenty-five years since then dissolved like smoke and she instinctively looked for the weal left by the button on the palm of her hand. She remembered not only all that he said and did but the complete suspension of *her* existence during that August week. I was not myself—they all told me so at the time. She remembered—but with one white burning blank as where acid has dropped on a photograph: *under no conditions* could she remember his face.

So, wherever he may be waiting, I shall not know him. You have no time to run from a face you do not expect.

The thing was to get to the taxi before any clock struck what could be the hour. She would slip down the street and round the side of the square to where the square gave on the main road. She would return in the taxi, safe, to her own door, and bring the solid driver into the house with her to pick up the parcels from room to room. The idea of the taxi driver made her decisive, bold: she unlocked her door, went to the top of the staircase and listened down.

She heard nothing—but while she was hearing nothing the *passé* air of the staircase was disturbed by a draught that travelled up to her face. It emanated from the basement: down there a door or window was being opened by someone who chose this moment to leave the house.

The rain had stopped; the pavements steamily shone as Mrs Drover let herself out by inches from her own front door into the empty street. The unoccupied houses opposite continued to meet her look with their damaged stare. Making towards the thoroughfare and the taxi, she tried not to keep looking behind. Indeed, the silence was so intense—one of those creeks of London silence exaggerated this summer by the damage of war—that no tread could have gained on hers unheard.

Where her street debouched on the square where people went
on living, she grew conscious of, and checked, her unnatural
pace. Across the open end of the square two buses impassively
passed each other: women, a perambulator, cyclists, a man
wheeling a barrow signalized, once again, the ordinary flow
of life. At the square's most populous corner should be—and
was—the short taxi rank. This evening, only one taxi—but
this, although it presented its blank rump, appeared already
to be alertly waiting for her. Indeed, without looking round
the driver started his engine as she panted up from behind
and put her hand on the door. As she did so, the clock struck
seven. The taxi faced the main road: to make the trip back to
her house it would have to turn—she had settled back on the
seat and the taxi *had* turned before she, surprised by its knowing movement, recollected that she had not 'said where'. She
leaned forward to scratch at the glass panel that divided the
driver's head from her own.

The driver braked to what was almost a stop, turned round
and slid the glass panel back: the jolt of this flung Mrs Drover
forward till her face was almost into the glass. Through the
aperture driver and passenger, not six inches between them,
remained for an eternity eye to eye. Mrs Drover's mouth hung
open for some seconds before she could issue her first scream.
After that she continued to scream freely and to beat with
her gloved hands on the glass all round as the taxi, accelerat-
ing without mercy, made off with her into the hinterland of
deserted streets.

Civilians and
War Workers

THE WALL

William Sansom (1912–1976)

Born into a well-to-do middle-class family, Sansom grew up and lived in London, though he studied in Germany for a time as a young man. His breakthrough as a writer came with his short stories about life in wartime London, first published in magazines such as *Penguin New Writing* and *Horizon* and subsequently collected in the volume *Fireman Flower and Other Stories* in 1944. 'The Wall' draws on his own experiences as a member of the National Fire Service in wartime London, and betrays the intensity of the Blitz and the peculiar, unreal atmosphere of the capital at war.

I T WAS OUR THIRD JOB THAT NIGHT.

Until this thing happened, work had been without inci-
dent. There had been shrapnel, a few enquiring bombs, and
some huge fires; but these were unremarkable and have since
merged without identity into the neutral maze office and noise
and water and night, without date and without hour, with
neither time nor form, that lowers mistily at the back of my
mind as a picture of the air-raid season.

I suppose we were worn down and shivering. Three a.m.
is a meanspirited hour. I suppose we were drenched, with the
cold hose water trickling in at our collars and settling down at
the tails of our shirts. Without doubt the heavy brass couplings
felt moulded from metal-ice. Probably the open roar of the
pumps drowned the petulant buzz of the raiders above, and
certainly the ubiquitous fire-glow made an orange stage-set
of the streets. Black water would have puddled the City alleys
and I suppose our hands and our faces were black as the water.
Black with hacking about among the burnt up rafters. These
things were an every-night nonentity. They happened and they
were not forgotten because they were never even remembered.

But I do remember it was our third job. And there we were—Len, Lofty, Verno and myself, playing a fifty-foot jet up the face of a tall city warehouse and thinking of nothing at all. You don't think of anything after the first few hours. You just watch the white pole of water lose itself in the fire and you think of nothing. Sometimes you move the jet over to another window. Sometimes the orange dims to black—but you only ease your grip on the ice-cold nozzle and continue pouring careless gallons through the window. You know the fire will fester for hours yet. However, that night the blank, indefinite hours of waiting were sharply interrupted—by an unusual sound. Very suddenly a long rattling crack of bursting brick and mortar perforated the moment. And then the upper half of that five-storey building heaved over towards us. It hung there, poised for a timeless second before rumbling down at us. I was thinking of nothing at all and then I was thinking of everything in the world.

In that simple second my brain digested every detail of the scene. New eyes opened at the sides of my head so that, from within, I photographed a hemispherical panorama bounded by the huge length of the building in front of me and the narrow lane on either side.

Blocking us on the left was the squat trailer pump, roaring and quivering with effort. Water throbbed from its overflow valves and from leakages in the hose and couplings. A ceaseless stream spewed down its grey sides into the gutter. But nevertheless a fat iron exhaust pipe glowed red-hot in the middle of the wet engine. I had to look past Lofty's face. Lofty was staring at the controls, hands tucked into his armpits for warmth. Lofty was thinking of nothing. He had a black diamond of soot over one eye, like the White-eyed Kaffir in negative.

To the other side of me was a free run up the alley. Overhead swung a sign—'Catto and Henley'. I wondered what in hell they sold. Old stamps? The alley was quite free. A couple of lengths of dead, deflated hose wound over the darkly glistening pavement. Charred flotsam dammed up one of the gutters. A needle of water fountained from a hole in a live hose-length. Beneath a blue shelter light lay a shattered coping stone. The next shop along was a tobacconist's, windowless, with fake display cartons torn open for anybody to see. The alley was quite free.

Behind me, Len and Verno shared the weight of the hose. They heaved up against the strong backward drag of water pressure. All I had to do was yell 'Drop it'—and then run. We could risk the live hose snaking up at us. We could run to the right down the free alley—Len, Verno and me. But I never moved. I never said 'Drop it' or anything else. That long second held me hypnotized, rubber boots cemented to the pavement. Ton upon ton of red-hot brick hovering in the air above us numbed all initiative. I could only think. I couldn't move.

Six yards in front stood the blazing building. A minute before I would never have distinguished it from any other drab Victorian atrocity happily on fire. Now I was immediately certain of every minute detail. The building was five storeys high.

The top four storeys were fiercely alight. The rooms inside were alive with red fire. The black outside walls remained untouched. And thus, like the lighted carriages of a night express, there appeared alternating rectangles of black and red that emphasized vividly the extreme symmetry of the window spacing: each oblong window shape posed as a vermilion panel set in perfect order upon the dark face of the wall. There were ten windows to each floor, making forty windows in all. In rigid rows of ten, one row placed precisely above the other, with strong contrasts of black and red, the blazing windows stood to attention in strict formation. The oblong building, the oblong windows, the oblong spacing. Orange-red colour seemed to *bulge* from the black frame-work, assumed tactile values, like boiling jelly that expanded inside a thick black squared grill.

Three of the storeys, thirty blazing windows and their huge frame of black brick, a hundred solid tons of hard, deep Victorian wall, pivoted over towards us and hung flatly over the alley. Whether the descending wall actually paused in its fall I can never know. Probably it never did. Probably it only seemed to hang there. Probably my eyes only digested its action at an early period of momentum, so that I saw it 'off true' but before it had gathered speed.

The night grew darker as the great mass hung over us. Through smoke-fogged fire-glow the moonlight had hitherto penetrated to the pit of our alley through declivities in the skyline. Now some of the moonlight was being shut out as the wall hung ever further over us. The wall shaded the moonlight like an inverted awning. Now the pathway of light above had been squeezed to a thin line. That was the only silver lining I ever believed in. It shone out—a ray of hope. But it was a declining hope, for although at this time the entire hemispherical scene appeared static, an imminence of movement could be sensed throughout—presumably because the scene was actually moving. Even the speed of the shutter which closed the photograph on my mind was powerless to exclude this motion from a deeper consciousness. The picture appeared static to the limited surface sense, the eyes and the material brain, but beyond that there was hidden movement.

The second was timeless. I had leisure to remark many things. For instance, that an iron derrick, slightly to the left, would not hit me. This derrick stuck out from the building and I could feel its sharpness and hardness as clearly as if I had run my body intimately over its contour. I had time to notice that it carried a foot-long hook, a chain with three-inch rings, two girder supports and a wheel more than twice as large as my head.

A wall will fall in many ways. It may sway over to the one side or the other. It may crumble at the very beginning of its fall. It may remain intact and fall flat. This wall fell as flat as a pancake. It clung to its shape through ninety degrees to the horizontal. Then it detached itself from the pivot and slammed down on top of us.

The last resistance of bricks and mortar at the pivot point cracked off like automatic gunfire. The violent sound both deafened us and brought us to our senses. We dropped the hose and crouched. Afterwards Verno said that I knelt slowly on one knee with bowed head, like a man about to be knighted. Well, I got my knighting. There was an incredible noise—a thunderclap condensed into the space of an eardrum—and then the bricks and the mortar came tearing and burning into the flesh of my face.

Lofty, away by the pump, was killed. Len, Verno and myself they dug out. There was very little brick on top of us. We had been lucky. We had been framed by one of those symmetrical, oblong window spaces.

NIGHT IN THE FRONT LINE

Molly Lefebure (1919–2013)

The daughter of a senior civil servant of French descent, Lefebure studied journalism at King's College London, and covered the Blitz and other stories as a junior reporter before taking up a job as secretary to a prominent forensic pathologist in 1941. Although she was sceptical about taking up potentially tedious secretarial work, she found that the job provided her with plenty of interesting (if also often gruesome) insights into human nature. Living to the age of 93, Lefebure was elected a Fellow of the Royal Society of Literature in 2010, three years before her death. 'Night in the Front Line' shows the acuity of Lefebure's skill for psychological observation, as it offers a nuanced picture of people's reactions to the Blitz and captures both the good and the bad impulses brought out under the stress of bombardment.

'ALF A MO, 'ITLER, 'ALF A MO,' SAID MRS MINNOW AS the remains of her former staircase descended upon her, burying her in a welter of wood, dust and plaster.

She struggled and groped in the darkness, her one thought to find the attaché case of valuables which she had placed handy when she had retired under the stairs for refuge at the commencement of the raid. As she groped she talked.

'Wot the b— 'ell. I've been bombed that's wot. Well, nothing like it. Where'd I put that case? Well I'll be blowed. 'Ere it is, just where I thought.' And clutching the case tightly she heaved, scrambled and fought her way out from the debris surrounding her, and stumbling over many unexpected and unseen obstacles for several desperate moments, found herself in the brick-littered street.

'I been bombed that's wot,' said Mrs Minnow once again. 'Lucky I'm not 'urt and lucky I was under them stairs.'

'You all right, ma?' said a man's voice. It was the warden. Mrs Minnow staunchly replied yes. He told her to wait a tick and disappeared again. Mrs Minnow, recovered from her first shock, was now able to take stock of the world about her. It was a very confused world. The night was furiously bloodstained by the blazing docks and quivering in the echoing blasphemy of the guns. Great flashes of searing gunfire rick-racked across the sky and the exploding shells burst there like burning and passionate kisses. Below this vast dome of sound and fury seethed a human clamour; shouting, crying, screaming, traffic hooting and ambulance bells clanging, footsteps racing in the dark; people colliding, searching, cursing, dying.

Mrs Minnow was most intensely aware of another sound which grew closer every minute… a steady, belly-thumping, rhythmic, slow, low throb, gaining upon the ear till it was directly overhead, beating the world out; then three long streaks of sound, like the tearing of three long strips of silk, and Mrs Minnow was crouching beside what had been left of her front doorstep, with the world rumbling, tumbling around her again. Another warden helped her up and she dusted herself down. She tried to say something appropriate to his kindness and the occasion, but only managed to gasp, 'Getting a bit too much if you ask me.'

'You all right?' asked the warden.

'Yes,' said Mrs Minnow.

'All right, you trot along to the school, they'll take care of you there. Mind the 'ose pipes.'

Clutching her case Mrs Minnow started to grope her way to the school. The pavements were littered with debris and hose pipes snaked across them. Now and then she was obliged to make detours. She overtook Mr and Mrs East, also bound for the school. Mrs East was weeping bitterly. Mr East carried the canary and wore his old straw hat.

''Ouse is gone,' he said laconically. 'Direct 'it on Mason's. All killed they say. Three little kids there.'

'It's a bloody shame to leave kids in this,' said Mrs Minnow. ''Ell it is, proper 'ell. Blimey, 'ere comes Jerry again.'

'Oh, never mind 'im,' said Mr East with superb scorn. 'Where was you, in the Anderson?'

'No, under the stairs. The others all went along to the Landers' Anderson... I say I 'ope they're all right... no, I was under the stairs. I'd took a look at the fire and didn't like the look of things so I went under the stairs. Always reckoned safe in the last war stairs was...'

'Bombs is different this war,' said Mr East. 'Where's old Jim?'

'Down at the docks 'elping put out the fire.'

'All that nice furniture gone and the nice new clock wot our Jack give us,' wailed Mrs East. 'Oh, lemme die, lemme die.'

'Now 'old on, Liza,' said Mr East. 'Cheer up, Liza. We're nearly there now. Oughta be glad you're alive you ought. Downright ungrateful that's wot you are.'

They came to the school. The big hall was crowded with people, most of them lying upon rugs and mattresses on the floor. The lights had gone out and lamps were being used. Somebody gave Mrs Minnow a cup of hot tea and a biscuit. She sat on a canvas stool drinking the tea and nibbling the biscuit.

'Don't think much of that biscuit,' she remarked presently to a small woman beside her. 'Government oughter be able to give us a better biscuit 'n that.'

'My Joey's gone,' said the small woman, in a monotonous voice. 'I've lost my Joey.'

'What 'appened, duck?' asked Mrs Minnow kindly.

'My Joey's gone,' said the small woman again. 'I've lost my Joey.'

'Nutty,' observed the stout lady on Mrs Minnow's right.

'You oughta go to 'ospital,' said Mrs Minnow to Joey's mother. 'Ain't there nobody to take care of 'er proper?' she asked.

'She'll be orright. We'll all be orright in the morning or else we'll be bleeding well dead.'

Mrs Minnow finished her biscuit and went in search of Mrs East. She was still weeping and did not respond to Mrs Minnow's kindly attentions. 'Blooming downpour,' said Mrs Minnow, a trifle disgusted. 'Blimey, I'll be glad to get outa this. Wot's the good of crying over spilt milk.' She felt cold and weary. The hall was packed with people and she found a place on the floor in the corridor. A woman with two small boys gave her a blanket to wrap up in.

'We was in a shelter,' she told Mrs Minnow. ''Ad our blankets there and our clothes.' She indicated the bulging pillowcases her children rested their heads upon. 'Blasted bomb dropped near the shelter. We was about the only ones to get out all right.'

'Musta been a nasty shock.'

'Not 'alf,' said the mother. She didn't say much more, but looked nervously at her children now and again. Mrs Minnow saw her extend a furtive hand and run it over the smallest child's slumbering body.

They lay there. It was chilly and dark. Around them the murmuring of many voices, sounds of broken weeping and low moaning. Heavy raucous snores. Again and again the engines of German planes thumping and circling overhead, the screaming of falling bombs, dull shattering explosions... Mrs Minnow's heart pounding in pulpy dread as she pressed her stout person as flat as possible against the hard unyielding floor as if she would burrow a shallow hole there and in it hide.

Presently, through sheer exhaustion, she slept. Her sleep was thick, murky and blotched with the dust of debris and the smoke of fire. She would suddenly start awake, to find her stomach cold and sick and her hip-bone sticking sharply into the floor. Then she would mutter, sigh heavily and sleep again.

In the early hours of the morning she was once more flung awake, her head splintering into many little pieces, her brain ripped into fragments by the agonized shrieking of many persons. Something stifling was pressing her down, there was a vast roaring and the sliding shaking of buildings collapsing.

Her first instinct was to lie quite still, while the floor seemingly tilted and retilted beneath her. Then it steadied. Something warm trickled down her left leg. A woman's voice yelled in agony. 'Get me out! Get me out!'

Mrs Minnow began to heave and struggle. She rose and fell in the debris like an ooze-embedded prehistoric monster reincarnating. More plaster, more dust, more splintering wood. After long suffocating moments of kicking and clawing, panting and groaning, a hand seized her shoulder and a rough voice said, ''Old on ma, we've got you.'

She emerged. She noticed, without realizing the full meaning of her escape, that a great lump of stone had fallen a few feet from her. Beside her, beneath broken rafter and rubbish, something moaned and moved. Her shivering mind recalled her case. She cried, 'My case, my case,' and tried to stoop to search for it in the dust and muck at her feet, but somebody took hold of her and led her into the playground. She sat on some stone steps. She felt inside her blouse where she had pinned her purse and old-age pension book and they were still there. She held her hands close to her face… inspected them… they were black with grime. She pulled up her torn skirt and looked at her leg; it bore a slight cut.

She sat very still. The guns thundered and exhorted; she paid them no heed. Then a picture flashed before her eyes, a sound cut her ears: the mother of the two little boys, following a man carrying one of them. She uttered strange shrill cries. Her face was white and open like a window when the curtains blow through. Her hands drooped in front of her, lacerated and bloodstained from her wild efforts to dig out her children.

Mrs Minnow recoiled. Then she got up. She was going to clear out of this. She was going to find a nice deep shelter and stay there till it was all over. Get away. Hide and get right away from it all. Her brain sagged as though the elastic had gone from an old pair of knickers. She mooched across the playground, down the street. She narrowly escaped being knocked over by an ambulance.

A policeman stopped her. 'Where are you going, mother?'

'A shelter,' said Mrs Minnow. 'I wanta shelter. A deep shelter.'

The policeman took her to a shelter; he was a kind man. Mrs Minnow descended into that humid atmosphere and there, huddled on a bench below ground, inert and motionless, she waited for the morning. When the All Clear sounded she ascended into the desolate, smoking, reeking wasteland which had been her world and was now a dark pile of ruins. She thought only of getting out of the place and going to her sister in Chingford. She felt dimly that first she should look for her old man, though what would be the good? However, she made her way towards the docks, but was stopped by a police barricade. She was told they were still putting out the fire. She turned to go back home, but remembered home was no more, and reaching the end of her street one glance told her it was of no use to stop there. She said to a warden she knew, 'If my Jim comes 'ome tell 'im I've gone to Elsie's at Chingford.'

The warden said he would.

She was given a lift on a coster's pony-cart to Bow Road. Here the coster met his brother's wife who was evacuating with his own family to Ilford, and as there was not enough room on the cart for them all Mrs Minnow was put down on the pavement, expressing her thanks and saying she hoped they would all meet again in better times. Then she walked on, along Bow Road to Stratford.

On either side walked people like herself; some wheeling their salvaged belongings in prams, others pushing little hand carts such as children play with in the streets, others carrying cases or stuffed pillow-cases, others just like Mrs Minnow with only themselves rescued from the bombs.

Along the roadway streamed a constant procession of little carts, cars, lorries, vans, conveying escaping families with their hastily snatched belongings; some had even managed to bring away bedding and furniture. Buses also passed, packed with paper-faced children.

A young woman carrying a baby and followed by a girl of ten and a little boy, struggling to bear between them a bulging old case, approached Mrs Minnow and asked, 'Got a pram?'

'No,' said Mrs Minnow.

'Know anybody 'oo 'as?'

'No.'

'This case is bleeding 'eavy,' said the young woman plaintively.

Mrs Minnow shook her head and walked on. She felt as though her feet would drop off and decided to hitch-hike, so she stopped on the kerb edge and raised a forlorn thumb to a passing lorry. It did not stop.

'Blooming 'ard-'earted un-Christian be'aviour,' said Mrs Minnow bitterly, turning to a young woman waiting at the nearby bus stop. The buses and trolley-buses were few and far between, and when they came they were filled to overflowing. Mrs Minnow tried boarding one or two but retired defeated. Suddenly she wanted to talk. To talk and go on talking. She turned once more to the young woman and recited her woes in a blank abandoned monologue.

'Bombed twice I been. Once in me own 'ouse... then in the school. School full of people... nearly all killed. Oh, terrible it's been, terrible. But I'm getting out of it, going to me sister's at Chingford. Couldn't bear another night I couldn't, drive me mad. Wouldn't go through that again not for a 'undred pounds. All night at it they was. Never stopped. All me 'ome gone. Not much I 'ad, but it was me little all. Everythink gone. Look at me. Look at the sight I am! Look at me 'ands! No water to wash 'em with. No light. No gas. Nothink left to me but me purse and pension book. Nothink. My God, what a blooming awful world it is.'

The young woman leapt at a passing bus and was borne away arguing violently with the exasperated conductor. Mrs Minnow stared vacantly after her, muttered, 'My God,' once more, then slowly turned to continue her journey to Chingford.

Another lorry approached. She hailed it dispiritedly, it drew up. It was carrying coals. The driver thrust out a blackened face.

'Give us a lift, mate,' said Mrs Minnow.

The driver hesitated. Then he opened the door of his driving-cabin. 'All right, ma,' he said. "Oist yerself up now. 'Ere, give us yer 'and.'

GRANDMA WAS A LAND GIRL

Frederick Burrows Urquhart (1912–1995)

Urquhart was a Scottish novelist and short story writer, and a prolific contributor to literary magazines in the 1930s and 1940s, including Cyril Connolly's new magazine *Horizon*. His work is characterized by recurring homosexual themes (which made his early novels difficult to place with publishers), reflecting Urquhart's own sexual orientation. Particularly in his short fiction, however, he also focused on women's experiences, often highlighting the plight of socially marginalized women. 'Grandma Was A Land Girl' is a rather cheerful, light-hearted example of his work, however, and draws on Urquhart's own wartime life: while his brothers enlisted, Urquhart was a conscientious objector who spent the war working as a farm labourer.

THE LITTLE OLD MAN CAME INTO THE DAIRY WHEN Jockie was getting the cans ready for the milking one Sunday afternoon. He had a thin brown face and he wore a shapeless paddy hat and a pair of shrunken flannel trousers that had been washed almost white. 'Ay, ay,' he said.

'Ay, ay,' Jockie said.

The little man looked about with curiosity. 'What a change there's been sin' I was here last. I hinna been at Dallow for twenty-five year.'

'Is that a fact?' Jockie said, shifting the cans beneath the milk cooler and placing the rubber tubes into them. 'Ye'll see a big difference. This new dairy and all the new byres.'

'Ay.' The little man stood with his hands in the pockets of his short trousers, rocking backwards and forwards. He gaped at the huge ten-gallon cans, at the white walls, at the zinc sinks, at the milk cooler, and finally at the sterilizing chest. 'What's that thing for?'

'That's the sterilizing chest,' Jockie said. 'Ye didna think it was a safe, did ye? We'd need an awfa lot o' money to fill that! We put the cans and things in there to be sterilized. We just turn on the steam and it does everything. See, that's the boiler house in there.'

'Oh, Jesus!' the wee man said, shaking his head in bewilderment. 'A sterilizing chest!'

He followed Jockie into the milking parlour. It was long and light, gleaming with cleanliness. The first batch of eighteen cows were already in their stalls beside the units, placidly munching dairy cake, waiting for the milking machine to be switched on. The little man stared at the machine, at the glass bowls for the milk, at the pipes running through to the dairy. 'Oh, Jesus!' he said, softly. 'What next!'

He watched the land girls go from cow to cow, wash their udders with the sponges attached to each unit, and then strip them into the strip-cups. 'What are they doin'?' he asked.

'Strippin' them to see that they hinna got mastitis or anythin' like that,' Jockie said. 'The udder must aye be washed afore they get milked. I dinna suppose they'd be as hygienic as that in the auld byres when you were here last.'

'Oh, Jesus!' the wee man said. 'Oh, Jesus!'

He walked slowly along the milking parlour, eyeing the land girls in their white overalls. Big Greta, looming up from behind a cow she had been stripping, winked at him. 'Hello, Big Boy!'

He stared at her. Greta grinned at Mary and pretended to go all coy. 'My fatal fascination!' she said, touching her hair with exaggerated femininity. She turned and pulled the handle of the hopper, sending the dairy cake rattling down into the trough. 'Come on, sweetheart, get your cake!' She slapped the cow on the haunch.

'What's that?' The little man nodded at the hopper.

'That's a hopper,' Greta said. 'The cake comes down through a hole in the loft. This handle releases it into the troughs.'

'Oh, Jesus!' the little man said.

'Ye'll ha'e to see the byres now,' Jockie said, winking at the girls. 'Come on and I'll show ye. The most up-to-date byres in this part o' Scotland.'

The little man stood open-mouthed in the centre of the first byre. 'It'll be nae bother to muck oot a place like this,' he said.

'Nae bother ava!' Jockie laughed.

'Oh, Jesus!' The little man shook his head solemnly. 'Fancy puttin' cows in a braw place like this! It's guid enough for fowk to bide in. Fancy lettin' cows in here to skitter aboot a' ower the place! Their names up on boards, too, and a bowl for each ane to drink oot o'… and such comfortable-like stalls! What are cows comin' til! Oh, Jesus!'

They went back into the parlour. The milking had started. The little man stood with his back to the wall and watched. There was a steady stream of cows entering and leaving the parlour; they came in at one door, went into the first vacant stall, stood while their udders were washed and the teat-cups attached, munched the cake while being milked and walked out when the gate of the stall was opened. Every cow was milked in four minutes. Just now, Jockie said to the little man, they were milking one hundred and fifteen in about an hour.

The usual Sunday afternoon spectators were beginning
to gather; they ranged along the wall of the milking parlour,
nodding at the machine and discussing it with each other. The
wee man talked to those nearest him. He kept shaking his head,
contrasting this method with the methods that had been used
when he was last at Dallow. Greta and Mary, who were working the units nearest to where he was standing, heard him say
'Oh, Jesus!' every now and then.

A young man started to chaff him. Greta heard him say: 'But
ye're nae regrettin' the passin' o' the auld byres, are ye? Ye're nae
wantin' to go back to the days o' "the Muckin' o' Geordie's Byre"?'

'Ah, there was a song for ye, now,' the wee man said sadly.
'It was a' in there. The verra words show it.' And he began to
sing in a mournful voice:

> 'A hunder years ha'e passed and mair,
> Where Sprottie's was the hill is bare,
> The croft's awa', so ye'll see nae mair
> The muckin' o' Geordie's byre.'

The young man nudged his neighbour and winked. They guf-
fawed ribaldly. But the wee man, his eyes raised to the ceiling,
looking at something far beyond the gleaming pipes of the
milking parlour, went on singing softly:

> 'His fowk's a' dead and awa' lang syne,
> So in case his memory we should tine,

Just whistle this tune to keep ye in min'
O' the muckin' o' Geordie's byre.'

He stood for a few minutes, shaking his head sadly. Then as if
coming out of a daze, he looked at the efficient white-clad land
girls, at the gleaming pipes, the sponges and the long red tubes.
'A factory!' he muttered. 'It's just like a factory! Oh, Jesus!' And
he turned and went out, mumbling to himself.

Greta gawked at Mary. Then she sagged at the knees. 'Oh,
Jee-SUS!'

Mary sighed sympathetically. 'It's not really funny, Greta.
Poor old man. Maybe we'd feel like him if we came back after
twenty-five years and saw all the changes.'

But Greta could not resist the temptation for some buf-
foonery. She leaned her elbow on a cow's haunch. 'If I do
come back I'll bring my grandchildren with me. They'll be
pushing my bath-chair. "Now, children, this is the farm where
Grandma was a land girl. Yes, children, don't laugh. Grandma
was a land girl once. Williamina!" She gave the cow a poke.
'"Stop picking your nose and pay attention to what Grandma
is saying. Now, we'll go into the milking parlour. Good gracious, what's this! My my, how things have changed since
Grandma was a girl! What have we here?"—I'll peer through
my lorgnette—"What's this? Do you mean to tell me, young
man, that you don't have any cows? You've never even heard
of cows? But we had cows here when I was a girl. Well do I
remember them! Especially number a hundred and nine, who

kicked like fun! Yes, children, Grandma still has the mark on her... well, anyway, she still has the mark! I'll maybe show you when you're older, Williamina, if you'll learn to stop picking your nose! Young man, do you mean to stand there and tell me brazenly that you have *no* cows?"'

Greta glared fiercely at Jockie, who held his sides, helpless with laughter. 'Do you mean that you have no byres to muck? That you don't even have land girls? Good gracious, what's the world coming to?' She shook her head indignantly, a fierce old lady to the life. 'But *where* do you get the milk?'

'We just make it with a puckle powder and water.' Jockie only managed to say this coherently before dissolving again into hysterical laughter.

'Oh, I see! It all comes out of tubes!'

Greta swooned against the cow, holding up her imaginary lorgnette. 'Oh, Jesus! And it's carried along from the tubes to the consumer by aeroplane! My my, how times have changed since Grandma was a land girl! Oh, Jee... sus!'

Combatants

I HAD TO GO SICK

Julian Maclaren-Ross (1912–1964)

Maclaren-Ross grew up in England and France, and started writing stories and scenarios for film scripts from a young age. Following a spell working as a salesman for vacuum cleaners and a period of unemployment, his career as an author took off properly with the publication of one of his short stories, 'A Bit of a Smash in Madras', in the then new magazine *Horizon*, in 1940. Serving at home before being dismissed from the army following a conviction for going absent without leave, Maclaren-Ross wrote and published several more wartime stories, later collected in *The Stuff to Give the Troops* (1944). In 'I had to go sick', Maclaren-Ross takes on army bureaucracy, which had already been the butt of many jokes in the First World War. His narrator's Kafkaesque journey through the army medical system reveals the seeming absurdities of army rules and regulations and illustrates the bewilderment felt by many of the new citizen soldiers drafted in for the duration of the war.

I HADN'T BEEN IN THE ARMY LONG AT THE TIME. ABOUT A week, not more. We were marching round the square one afternoon and I couldn't keep in step. The corporal kept calling out 'Left, left!' but it didn't do any good. In the end the corporal told me to fall out. The platoon sergeant came rushing up and said: 'What the hell's wrong with you, man! Why can't you hold the step?'

I didn't know, I couldn't tell him. There was an officer on the square, and the sergeant-major, and they were both watching us.

'Got anything wrong with your leg?' the sergeant said. 'Your left leg?'

'I've got a scar on it, Sergeant,' I told him.

'Dekko,' the sergeant said.

So I rolled up my trouser leg and showed him the scar on my knee. The sergeant looked at it and shook his head. 'That don't look too good, lad,' he said. 'How'd you come to get it?'

'I was knocked down by a bike. Years ago.'

By this time the sergeant-major had come up and he looked at the scar too. 'What's your category, lad?' he asked me. 'A1?'

'Yes, sir.'

'Well, you go sick tomorrow morning and let the M.O. have a look at that leg. Meantime sit in that shed over there till it's time to fall out.'

There was a Bren Gun lesson going on in the shed when I got there. My arrival interrupted it. 'Who the hell are you?' the N.C.O. taking the lesson asked me. 'What d'you want?'

'I've been sent over here to sit down, Corporal.'

'To sit down?'

'Sergeant-major sent me.'

'Oh, well, if he sent you that's all right. But don't go opening your trap, see? Keep mum and don't say nothing.'

'Very good, Corporal.'

'Not so much of it,' the corporal said.

The lesson went on. I listened but couldn't understand what it was all about. I'd never seen a Bren Gun before. And then the corporal's pronunciation didn't help matters. I sat there in the shed until everyone else had fallen out. Then the sergeant-major came over to me.

'Fall out,' he said. 'What're you waiting for. Parade's over is the day, you're dismissed. And don't forget—you go tomorrow morning,' he shouted after me.

'How do I go sick?' I asked the other fellows, back in the barrack-room.

They didn't know, none of them had ever been sick. 'Ask the Sarnt,' they said.

But I couldn't find the sergeant, or the corporal either. They'd gone off to a dance in the town. So I went down to the

cookhouse and there was an old sweat sitting on a bucket outside, peeling spuds. You could see he was an old sweat because
he was in shirtsleeves and his arms were tattooed all over. So I
asked him how to go sick, and he said: 'Ah, swinging the lead,
eh? M.O.'ll mark you down in red ink, likely.'

'What happens if he does that?'

'C.B. for a cert. Scrubbing, or mebbe a spot of spud bashing.
You won't get less than seven days, anyhow.'

'What, seven days' C.B. for going sick?'

'Sure, if you're swinging the lead. Stands to reason. There
ain't nothing wrong with you now, is there? A1, aintcher?'

'Yes.'

'There you are then. You'll get seven all right,' said the
sweat. 'What d'you expect? All you lads are alike, bleeding
lead swingers the lot of you.'

He spat on the ground and went on peeling spuds. I could
see he wasn't going to say any more so I walked on. Further
along I stopped by another old sweat. This second sweat was
even older and more tattooed than the first one. And he hadn't
any teeth.

'Excuse me,' I said, 'can you tell me how to go sick?'

'Go sick?' said this second, toothless sweat. 'You don't want
to do that, cocker. Christ, you don't want to do that.'

'Why not?' I said.

'Well, look at me. Went sick I did with a pain in the
guts, and what's the M.O. do? Silly bleeder sent me down
the Dental Centre and had them take all me teeth out. I ask

you, do it make bleeding sense? Course it don't. You got the guts ache and they pull out all your teeth. Bleeding silly. And they ain't given me no new teeth neither, and here I been waiting six munce. No,' said the sweat, 'you don't want to go sick. Take my tip, lad: keep away from that there M.O. long as you can.'

'But I've got to go sick. I've been ordered to.'

'Who by?'

'Sergeant-major.'

'What's wrong with you?'

'My leg, so they say.'

'Your leg? Then mebbe they'll take your teeth out too. Ain't no knowing what they'll do once they start on you. I'm bleeding browned-off with the bleeding sick I am.'

'Well, how do I go about it?'

'See your Orderly Sarnt. Down Company Office. He's the bloke you want.'

On the door of the Orderly Sergeant's bunk it said *Knock and wait*. I did both and a voice shouted: 'Come in, come in. Don't need to bash the bleeding door down.'

There was a corporal sitting at a table covered with a blanket writing laboriously on a sheet of paper.

'Yeh?' he said, looking up. 'What d'you want?'

'I was looking for the Orderly Sergeant,' I said.

'I'm the Orderly Sergeant,' said the corporal. 'State your business and be quick about it. I ain't got all night.'

'I want to go sick, Sergeant. I mean Corporal.'

'Don't you go making no smart cracks here,' said the corporal. 'And stand properly to attention when you speak to an N.C.O.'

'Sorry, Corporal.'

'Ain't no such word in the British Army,' the corporal told me. 'Now what's your name? Age? Service? Religion? Medical category? Okay, you parade outside here eight-thirty tomorrow morning. On the dot.'

I went to go out, but the corporal called me back. 'Here, half a mo. How d'you spell Picquet? One K or two?'

'No K's at all, Corporal,' I told him.

'Listen; didn't I tell you not to be funny? I'll stick you on a chitty, so help me, if you ain't careful. How d'you mean, no K's. How can you spell Picquet without no K's?'

I explained. The corporal looked suspicious. 'Sure? You ain't trying to be funny?'

'No, Corporal. P-i-c-q-u-e-t.'

'Okay.' He wrote it down. 'Need a bleeding dictionary to write this bastard out,' he muttered, and then looking up: 'All right, what're you waiting for? Scram! Gillo! And don't forget 0830 tomorrow. Bring your small kit in case.'

I didn't like to ask him in case of what. I got out quick before he gave me scrubbing or spud-bashing or tried to take my teeth out maybe.

I didn't sleep too well that night, I can tell you. Next morning at 0830 there I was outside the orderly sergeant's bunk with my small kit: I'd found out from our sergeant what that was.

There were quite a lot of other fellows there as well. It's funny how they pass you A1 into the Army and then find out you're nothing of the sort. One of these fellows had flat feet, another weak lungs and a third reckoned he was ruptured.

After awhile the corporal came out. 'All right,' he said. 'Get fell in, the sick.'

We fell in and were marched down to the M.I. Room.

'Keep in step, you!' the corporal shouted at me. 'Christ, can't you keep step?'

Down at the M.I. Room it said on the walls *No Smoking, No Spitting,* and we sat around waiting for our names to be called out. At last mine was called and I went in. The M.O. looked up. 'Yes, what's wrong with you?'

I looked round. There were two fellows standing behind me waiting their turn. A third was putting on his trousers in a corner. More crowded in the doorway behind. I felt silly with all these fellows listening in. I didn't know what to say.

'Come on, out with it,' said the M.O. 'Or perhaps it's something you'd rather say in private?'

'Well, sir, I would prefer it.'

'Right. Come back at five tonight.'

I went out again.

'What'd you get?' the orderly sergeant asked me.

'He said to come back at five, Corporal.'

'What's wrong? Got the clap?'

'No, Corporal.'

'Crabs, maybe?'

'No, not crabs.'

'Well, what the hell you want to see him in private for, then? Only blokes with V.D. see him in private as a rule. Unless they've crabs.'

At five I reported back to the M.I. Room.

'Right,' said the medical corporal. 'This way. Cap off. Don't salute.'

The M.O. said: 'Ah yes. Sit down and tell me all about it.'

I did. He seemed a bit disappointed that I hadn't V.D., but in the end he examined my leg.

'Does it hurt! No? What about if you kneel on it? H'm, yes, there's something wrong there. You'd better see the specialist. Report here tomorrow at ten.'

The specialist was at a hospital some miles away from the camp. He said: 'Try and straighten the leg. What, you can't? All right. Put your trousers on and wait outside.'

Pretty soon an orderly came out with a chitty. 'You're to have treatment twice a week,' he told me. 'Electrical massage. This way.'

I followed him down a lot of corridors and finally out into the grounds and up some steps into a hut with *Massage* on a board outside it. There I lay down on a table and a nurse strapped some sort of pad on my thigh. After that they gave me a series of shocks from an electric battery. It lasted about half an hour.

'Feeling better?' the nurse asked me when it was over.

'No,' I said.

I could hardly walk.

'That'll wear off by and by,' said the nurse.

I drove back in an ambulance to the M.I. Room.

'Had your treatment?'

'Yes, sir.'

The M.O. started to write something on a piece of paper. I was a bit nervous in case he used the red ink. But he didn't after all. He used blue ink instead. 'Give this to your Orderly Sergeant,' he said.

On the piece of paper it said 'Att. C.'

'Attend C!' said the orderly sergeant. 'Cor, you got it cushy, ain't you?'

'What's it mean, Corporal?' I asked.

'Attend C? Excused all duties. Bleeding holiday, that's what it amounts to.'

'Excused all duties,' the other fellows said in the barrack-room. 'You lucky cowson. With a bleeding march coming off tomorrow and all.'

Two days later I went to the hospital again. After a week or two of the treatment I'd developed quite a limp. The fellows all said I was swinging the lead. I limped about the camp doing nothing, in the intervals of having more electric shocks. Then, after about three weeks the M.O. sent for me again.

'Is your leg any better now?'

'No, sir,' I said.

'Treatment not doing you any good?'

'No, sir.'

'H'm. Well, I'd better put you down for a medical board in that case.'

So I didn't even go to the hospital any more. I used to lie on my bed all day long reading a book. But I got tired of that because I only had one book and I wasn't allowed out owing to being on sick. There weren't any other books in the camp. Meanwhile the fellows were marching and drilling and firing on the range, and the man in the next bed to me suddenly developed a stripe. This shook me, so I thought I'd go and see the sergeant-major.

I was a bit nervous when I got to his office. The sergeant-major had an alarming appearance. He looked almost exactly like an ape. Only he'd less hair on him, of course. But he was quite a decent fellow really.

When I came in he was telling two clerks and an A.T.S. girl how he'd nailed a native's hand to his desk during his service in India. He broke off this recital when he saw me standing there. 'Yes, lad, what d'you want?'

I explained that I was waiting for a medical board and meantime had nothing to do, as I was excused parades.

'But d'you *want* something to do?' the sergeant-major asked. He seemed stupefied.

'Yes, sir,' I said. 'I didn't join the Army to do nothing all day.'

The two clerks looked up when I said that, and the A.T.S. stared at me with her mouth open. The sergeant-major breathed heavily through his nose. Then he said: 'Can you use a typewriter, lad?'

'Yes, sir,' I said.

'Ah!' He jumped up from his table. 'Then sit you down here and show us how to use this ruddy thing. It's only just been sent us, see, and none of us know how to make the bleeder go.'

It was a very old typewriter, an Oliver. I'd used one before, so I didn't find it too difficult. Soon I was typing out long lists of names and other stuff full of initials and abbreviations that I didn't know the meaning of. Sometimes I couldn't read the handwriting, especially if one of the officers had written it, but the A.T.S. used to translate for me.

Then one day the Company Commander walked in.

'Who's this man?' he said, pointing at me with his stick.

'Sick man, sir,' the sergeant-major said. 'Waiting a medical board.'

'Well, he can't wait for it here. We're not allowed any more clerks. You've enough clerks already,' and he walked out again, after hitting my table a whack with his stick.

'All right, fall out,' the sergeant-major said to me. 'Back to your bunk.'

'Now we've no one to work the typewriter,' he said. 'Have to do it all by hand. Hell!'

Next day the orderly sergeant told me to go sick again. I'd got used to it by now. The other fellows called me the M.O.'s right marker.

This time it was a new M.O.: the other one had been posted elsewhere.

'Well, what's wrong with you?' he said.

I explained my case all over again.

'Let's see your leg.' He looked at it for a moment and then said: 'Well, there's nothing wrong with that, is there?'

'Isn't there, sir!'

'No.' He poked at the scar, seized hold of my leg, bent it, straightened it a few times and then looked puzzled. 'H'm. There is something wrong after all. You'd better have a medical board.'

'I'm down for one already, sir.'

'What? Well why the devil didn't you say so then? Wasting my time. All right. You can go now.'

In the morning the orderly sergeant came into our hut. 'Get your small kit together,' he said, 'and be down the M.I. Room in ten minutes. You're for a medical board. It come through just now.'

At the hospital I sat for some time in a waiting-room and nobody came near me. It was another hospital, not the one I used to go to for treatment. Then at last an officer came in. I stood up. He was a colonel.

'Carry on, carry on,' he said, and smiled very kindly. 'What's *your* trouble, eh?'

'I'm waiting for a medical board, sir.'

'A medical board? What for?'

'I have trouble with my knee, sir.'

'Oh? What happens? Does it swell up?'

'No, sir.'

'What, no swelling? H'm. Well, come with me, we'll soon

have you fixed up.' I followed this kindly colonel to the reception desk. 'Take this man along to Ward 9,' he told an orderly.

So I went along to Ward 9 and all the beds in it were empty except for one man sitting up in bed doing a jig-saw puzzle.

'Wotcher, mate,' this man said. 'What you got? Ulcers, maybe?'

'Ulcers? No,' I said.

'I got ulcers,' the man said. 'Stomach ulcers. Can't keep nothing down. Everything I eat comes up. Nothing but milk, and even that come up sometimes. It ain't no fun having ulcers, believe me, mate.'

'I can imagine that,' I said.

Then a nurse came in. 'Ah, you're the new patient. This way to the bathroom. Here are the pyjamas you change into afterwards.'

'Pyjamas?' I said.

'Yes,' said the nurse. 'And directly you've bathed and got your pyjamas on you hop into this bed here,' and she pointed to one next to the man with ulcers.

'But I don't want to go to bed,' I said. 'I'm not a bed patient. There's nothing wrong with me.'

'Then why are you here?'

'Nothing wrong with me like that, I mean. I'm waiting for a medical board.'

'Oh. Wait here a moment, please.' She fetched the orderly. The orderly said: 'S.M.O.'s orders he was to be brought here. Said it hisself. The S.M.O. Ward 9, he said.'

'But this ward is for gastric cases,' the nurse said. 'This man—isn't a gastric case.'

'I don't know nothing about that,' the orderly told her, and he went off.

The nurse said: 'There's some mistake. I'll see about it while you have your bath.'

So I had a bath, and when I came out she gave me some blue clothes and a shirt and a red tie to put on and said I needn't go to bed. 'You'll have to stay here until we get this straightened out,' she said. 'Would you like anything to eat?'

'I would, thank you, Nurse.'

'Well, there's only milk pudding. This ward's for gastrics, you see.'

'You won't get very fat on that, mate,' the man with ulcers said.

He was right. I ate two lots of milk pudding but still felt hungry afterwards. Then later on the M.O. came round. A lieutenant, he was. Quite young. He looked at my leg and said: 'This man's a surgical case, Nurse. What's he doing in here?'

'S.M.O.'s orders, Doctor.'

'Oh. Well, he'll have to stay here then.'

'How long will it be before I get this medical board, sir?' I said.

'Medical board? Might be months. Meantime you stay here.'

'Can I have something to eat besides milk pudding then, sir?'

'Yes. You can have chicken. Give him some chicken, Nurse.'

So he went away and I ate the chicken.

'Wish I was you, mate,' said the man with ulcers.

It wasn't so bad being in the hospital except that you only got eight-and-six on pay day. Every morning I used to go down to the massage department. 'Electrical massage is no good for your trouble,' said the M.O. 'We'll try ordinary massage.' So I had ordinary massage and then sat on a table with a weight tied to my leg swinging it to-and-fro.

'Now I know what swinging the lead means,' I said.

I used to have to lie down for two hours a day to recover from the treatment. I was limping quite heavily by the time the M.O. put his head in one morning and said: 'You're for a Board today. Twelve o'clock down in my office.'

I waited outside the office nervously, I thought they might order me to have my teeth out. But they didn't. I was called in and there were three medical officers, one a lieutenant-colonel, who asked me a lot of questions and examined my leg, and then I went back to the ward.

'How'd you get on, mate?' asked the ulcers-man. 'What'd they do?'

'I don't know,' I said. 'They didn't tell me.'

But that evening the M.O. came in and said: 'You've been graded B2.'

'What does that mean, sir?'

'Garrison duties at home and abroad.'

'Can I go back to the camp then, sir?'

'Not until the papers come through.'

A few days later he sent for me. In his office. 'Something's gone wrong,' he said. 'We've slipped up. It seems you should have seen the surgical specialist before having the Board. But you didn't, so these papers aren't valid. You'll have to have another Board now.'

'When'll that be, sir?'

'*I* don't know. Don't ask me.'

So that afternoon I saw the surgical specialist. He was a major, although he seemed quite young. He was very nice and cheerful and laughed a lot.

'Lie down on the table,' he said. 'That's right. Relax. Now bend the knee. Now straighten it. Hold it. Hold it. Try to hold it steady. Ha, ha! You can't, can you? Ha, ha! Of course you can't. You've got no tendon in it, that's why. The patella tendon. It's bust. How long ago did you say the accident…? Sixteen years? Good lord, nothing we can do about it now. You'll have to be awfully careful, though. No running, no jumping. If you were to jump down into a trench your leg'd snap like a twig. Can't understand how they ever passed you A1. Ha, ha! Well, I'll make my report on you right away. Oughtn't to be in the infantry with a leg like that at all.'

I went back to Ward 9. It was supper time. Junket.

'Can't keep it down,' said the man with ulcers, and he proved this by bringing it up again.

Well then the M.O. went on leave.

'Now you stay here,' he told me, 'until the next Board comes off. Don't suppose it'll be till I'm back from my seven days. Meantime you stay put.'

'Yes, sir,' I said.

But in the morning a new M.O. came round. He was a captain. With him was the matron. 'Stand by your beds!' he called out as he came in.

The ward had filled up in the last week or two, but most of the patients were in bed, so they couldn't obey. The five of us who were up came belatedly to attention.

'Bad discipline in this ward, Matron,' the captain said. 'Very slack. Who's the senior N.C.O. here?'

There was only one N.C.O. among the lot of us: a lance-corporal. He was up, as it happened, so he came in for an awful chewing-off.

'You've got to keep better order than this, Corporal,' said the captain. 'See that the men pay proper respect to an officer when he enters the ward. If I've any further cause for complaint I shall hold you responsible. Also the beds aren't properly in line. I'm not satisfied with this ward, not satisfied at *all*. I hope to see some improvement when I come round tomorrow. Otherwise…'

He walked on round the beds examining the patients in turn. The ward was electrified. He ordered most of the bed patients to get up and those who were up to go to bed. Except the lance-corporal, who had to keep order, and me. As for the man with ulcers, he was ordered out of the ward altogether. I was last on the list, standing by the end bed, when he came up.

'This man is fit to return to his unit, Matron,' he said when he'd looked at me.

'But he's awaiting a medical board, Doctor,' the matron said.

'Well, he can wait for it at his unit. We're not running a home for soldiers awaiting medical boards. I never heard of such a thing.'

'Lieutenant Jackson said…'

'Never mind what he said. I'm in charge here now, and I've just given an order. This man will return to his unit forthwith.'

Then he walked out and the matron went too. Two nurses came in and helped the man with ulcers into a wheel-chair. 'So long, mates,' he said, then they wheeled him away. I don't know what became of him: he just disappeared. After that we straightened the beds and got them all in line.

'Keep order!' said the lance-corporal. 'Why the hell should I keep order? I'm not an N.C.O. no more, they'll revert me soon's I get back. I'm Y Listed, see? A bloody private, so why should I bother? Bleeding sauce!'

I wondered when they were going to chuck me out. Forthwith, he'd said, and forthwith turned out to be the next day.

I left about two o'clock. In a lorry. It dropped me at the station and I'd two hours to wait for a train. At last I got back to the camp and it looked all changed somehow, with no one about. Everything seemed shut up. I reported to the orderly sergeant's bunk. Sitting in it was a corporal I'd never seen before.

'Who're you?' he said. 'What d'you want?'

I told him.

'No one told us you was coming,' said this new corporal, scratching his head. 'All the others have cleared off. Jerry been bombing the camp, see? We've been evacuated. Last draft leaves tomorrow.'

'Am I on it?'

'You'll be on it all right.'

'Well, where do I sleep? And what about my kit?'

'That'll be in the stores, I suppose. Buggered if I know. I'm from another company, I don't know nothing about you. Wait here, I'll see the storeman.'

But the storeman was out, and the stores were locked up. The corporal came back scratching his head.

'Buggered if I know when he'll be back. Gone on the piss, I shouldn't wonder. You better find a place to kip down. Here's a coupla blankets, if that's any use to you.'

Eventually I found a barrack-room that wasn't locked: all the other huts were closed up. There were two other blokes in this room, both out of hospital. 'Where're we going to, mate?' they asked me.

'Damned if I know.'

'Nobody bloody well does know, that's the rub.'

At last, after a lot of conjecture, we dossed down for the night. It was autumn by now and turning cold, and my two blankets didn't keep me very warm. I slept in all my clothes. Jerry came over during the night but didn't drop any bombs, or if he did we didn't hear them.

Then in the morning the corporal appeared. 'I've found some of your kit,' he said. We went down to the stores. There wasn't much of my kit left. Most of it had been pinched. My overcoat was gone and another one, much too small, left in its place.

'I don't know nothing about it,' said the storeman.

'You better get some breakfast,' the corporal said. 'I'll sort this lot out for you.'

Breakfast was a bacon sandwich, all the cookhouse fires had been let out.

'Bloody lark this is, ain't it?' said the cooks.

'You're telling us,' we said.

Then we paraded on the square, about forty of us. Don't know where all the others came from. Other companies, I suppose. A lieutenant was in charge of us.

'Where's your equipment?' he asked me.

'I've never been issued with it, sir,' I said.

'Never been issued with equipment!'

'No, sir. I was excused parades. And then I've just got out of hospital. I have the papers here, sir, that they gave me.'

'Oh, all right. I'll take charge of them.' He took the long envelope from me. Then a sergeant turned up and shouted: ''Shun! By the left, quick—*March*!'

We started off.

'Keep in step, there!' the sergeant shouted at me. 'Can't you keep in step? What the hell's the matter with yer!'

'I'm excused marching, Sergeant,' I said. 'I've just come from hospital.'

'Oh. All right, lad. Fall out. Wait here.' He went up to the officer and saluted. 'Scuse me, sir, there's a man here excused marching, sir.'

'What's that? Excused marching? Well he'll have to bloody-well march. This isn't a convalescent home.'

'It's five miles to the station, sir.'

'Oh, well, damn it, what d'you want done? Shove him on a truck or something. *Can't march,* indeed! He'd march soon enough if Jerry was after him.'

So the sergeant told a truck to stop and helped me to board it. It was full of kits and very uncomfortable, I nearly fell off twice. I felt a mass of bruises when we got to the station, and my leg had begun to ache. I sat down on a trolley and waited for the train to come in. It didn't come in for an hour, and the men, who'd marched up meantime, stood around and argued about where we were going. Some said Egypt, but others said No, because we weren't in tropical kit. So then they said Scotland and *then* Egypt. I personally didn't care where we were going, I was fed-up with the whole business, and my leg ached badly: I'd hit my bad knee getting down from the truck.

Then the train came in and it turned out to be full of recruits from another regiment going to wherever we were going, a new camp somewhere or other, and so we'd nowhere to sit. We stood for a long time in the corridor and then I tried sitting on my kit, but that wasn't a success because fellows kept falling over me and one of them kicked my bad leg. I was pretty browned-off by this time, so I got up and was going to sock him, but another chap got in front of me and said: 'You can't hit a sick man.'

'Who's a sick man?' I said. 'I'm a sick man.'

'So am I,' said the man I wanted to sock. 'I'm sick too. Hell, I got a hernia so bad they daren't operate. I'm waiting my ticket.'

'Sorry, mate,' I said. 'I didn't know.'

'That's okay,' he said, so we shook hands and he gave me some chocolate out of his haversack: we'd got bloody hungry by now.

'What about some grub?' everyone was saying. 'Where's the grub?'

By and by it came round in tins. A sergeant brought it.

'What's this?' we said.

'Beans. Take one.'

'Where's the meat?'

'You've had it,' said the sergeant. Everyone cursed. Then an officer came round, a captain. 'Any complaints?'

'What about some more food, sir,' we said.

'There isn't any. I've had none myself,' he said. 'Mistake somewhere.'

'You're telling us,' we said, but not to him.

It was dark when we got to this other town and the searchlights were up overhead. We formed up outside the station. Our sergeant appeared and recognized me. 'I'll see to you in a minute,' he said. But he couldn't, because all the transport had already gone. So I had to march after all. It was three miles, and after all that standing about I felt done in when we got to the new camp. We had a hot meal and I'd have slept like the dead if Jerry hadn't dropped a bomb somewhere near the barracks and woken me up.

'Bugger it,' I said. 'Now we'll have to go to the trenches.'

But they didn't blow the alarm after all, so we went off to sleep again.

In the morning I was down for sick, but the M.O. at this camp proved to be a much tougher proposition than any I'd yet encountered.

He said: 'What d'you mean, you've had a medical board? How can you have had a medical board? Where're your papers?'

'I gave them to the officer in charge of the draft, sir,' I said.

'Well, *I* haven't got them. What was the officer's name?'

'I don't know, sir.'

'You don't know. My God, you give your papers to an officer and you don't even know his name.' The M.O. held his head in his hands. 'God deliver me,' he said, 'from such idiocy!'

'I don't think I'm especially idiotic, sir,' I said.

'Your opinion of yourself is entirely irrelevant,' said the M.O. 'And you must remember to whom you're talking.'

'Yes, sir,' I said.

'Silence!' said the medical corporal, who'd come up at this.

The M.O. said: 'Now what's all this nonsense about a medical board? What happened? Were you re-graded?'

'Yes, sir. B2.'

'Let's see your pay-book. Corporal, get his A.B.64 Part I.'

I produced my pay-book.

'Not in it, sir,' said the corporal. 'A1 it says here.'

'I know,' I said, 'but...'

'Silence!' said the corporal. 'Speak only when you're spoken to.'

The M.O. had his head in his hands again. 'All this shouting,' he said. 'If that man gives any more trouble you'll have to charge him, Corporal.'

'Yes, sir,' said the corporal.

'Now listen,' the M.O. said to me, speaking very quietly. 'You say you've had a medical board, You say you've been re-graded. Well, you haven't. It's not in your pay-book. Therefore you've not been re-graded at all. You're lucky not to be charged with stating a falsehood, understand? Now don't come here again with any more nonsensical stories or you'll find yourself in trouble. Corporal, march this man out.'

'But, sir...' I said.

'Come on, you!' the corporal said. So I went. Two days later we started training, and the new sergeant found out I couldn't march and sent me sick again. It was another M.O. this time and he had my papers, they'd turned up again, and he said I've got to have another medical board.

That was a month ago, and I'm still waiting. I've not done much training so far, and I've had to pay for all the kit I had pinched at the other camp, and all I hope is this: that when they give me the Board, I don t have to go sick any more afterwards. I don't care if they grade me Z2 or keep me A1, so long as I don't have to go sick. I've had enough of it. I'm fed-up.

THE ORANGE GROVE

Alun Lewis (1915–1944)

Lewis was a Welsh poet and writer of short fiction from a poor mining community. A teacher when the war broke out, he joined the army in early 1940 and, after a period of training at home, was sent to British India with a commission in the South Wales Borderers. His wartime work chronicles both the transformation of civilians into soldiers and his subsequent experiences of warfare overseas. Stationed overseas, Lewis was profoundly troubled by his unfaithfulness to his wife Gweno, as he had fallen in love with a married woman, Freda Aykroyd, in India, and he ended his own life in Burma in March 1944.

T HE GREY TRUCK SLOWED DOWN AT THE CROSSROADS and the Army officer leaned out to read the sign post. *Indians Only,* the sign pointing to the native town read. *Dak Bungalow* straight on. 'Thank God,' said Staff-Captain Beale. 'Go ahead, driver.' They were lucky, hitting a dak bungalow at dusk. They'd bivouaced the last two nights, and in the monsoon a bivouac is bad business. Tonight they'd be able to strip and sleep dry under a roof, and heat up some bully on the Tommy cooker. Bloody good.

These bungalows are scattered all over India on the endless roads and travellers may sleep there, cook their food, and pass on. The rooms are bare and whitewashed, the veranda has room for a camp bed, they are quiet and remote, tended for the Government only by some old khansama or chowkey, usually a slippered and silent old Moslem. The driver pulled in and began unpacking the kit, the dry rations, the cooker, the camp bed, his blanket roll, the tin of kerosene. Beale went off to find the caretaker, whom he discovered squatting amongst the flies by the well. He was a wizened yellow-skinned old man in a soiled dhoti. Across his left breast was a plaster, loose and dripping with pus, a permanent discharge it seemed. He wheezed as he replied to the brusque request and raised himself with pain, searching slowly for his keys.

Beale came to give the driver a hand while the old man fumbled with the crockery indoors.

'The old crow is only sparking on one cylinder,' he said. 'Looks like T.B.', he added with the faint overtone of disgust which the young and healthy feel for all incurable diseases. He looked out at the falling evening, the fulgurous inflammation among the grey anchorages of cloud, the hot creeping prescience of the monsoon.

'I don't like it tonight,' he said. 'It's eerie; I can't breathe or think. This journey's getting on my nerves. What day is it? I've lost count.'

'Thursday, sir,' the driver said, 'August 25.'

'How d'you know all that?' Beale asked, curious.

'I have been thinking it out, for to write a letter tonight,' the driver said. 'Shall I get the cooker going, sir? Your bed is all ready now.'

'O.K.' Beale said, sitting on his camp bed and opening his grip. He took out a leather writing pad in which he kept the notes he was making for Divisional H.Q., and all the letters he'd received from home. He began looking among the letters for one he wanted. The little dusty driver tinkered with the cooker. Sometimes Beale looked up and watched him, sometimes he looked away at the night.

This place seemed quiet enough. The old man had warned

him there was unrest and rioting in the town. The lines had
been cut, the oil tanks unsuccessfully attacked, the court house
burnt down, the police had made lathi charges, the district
magistrate was afraid to leave his bungalow. The old man had
relished the violence of others. Of course you couldn't expect
the 11th to go by without some riots, some deaths. Even in this
remote part of Central India where the native princes ruled
from their crumbling Moghul forts through their garrisons
of smiling crop-headed little Gurkhas. But it seemed quiet
enough here, a mile out of the town. The only chance was
that some one might have seen them at the crossroads—it
was so sultry, so swollen and angry, the sky, the hour. He felt
for his revolver.

He threw the driver a dry box of matches from his grip.
Everything they carried was fungoid with damp, the driver
had been striking match after match on his wet box with
a curious depressive impassivity. Funny little chap, seemed
to have no initiative, as if some part of his will were para-
lysed. Maybe it was that wife of his he'd talked about the
night before last when they had the wood fire going in the
hollow. Funny. Beale had been dazed with sleep, half listening,
comprehending only the surface of the slow, clumsy words.
Hate. Hate. Beale couldn't understand hate. War hadn't
taught it to him, war was to him only fitness, discomfort,
feats of endurance, proud muscles, a career, irresponsible
dissipations, months of austerity broken by 'blinds' in Cairo,
or Durban, Calcutta or Bangalore or Bombay. But this little

rough-head with his soiled hands and bitten nails, his odd blue eyes looking away, his mean bearing, squatting on the floor with kerosene and grease over his denims—he had plenty of hate.

… 'tried to emigrate first of all, didn't want to stay any-where. I was fourteen, finished with reformatory schools for keeps… New Zealand I wanted to go. There was a school in Bristol for emigrants… I ran away from home but they didn't bother with me in Bristol, nacherly… Police sent me back. So then I become a boy in the Army, in the drums, and then I signed on. I'm a time-serving man, sir; better put another couple of branches on the fire; so I went to Palestine, against the Arabs; seen them collective farms the Jews got there, sir? Oranges… then I come home, so I goes on leave… We got a pub in our family and since my father died my mother been keeping it… for the colliers it is… never touch beer myself, my father boozed himself to death be'ind the counter. Well, my mother 'ad a barmaid, a flash dame she was, she was good for trade, fit for an answer any time, and showing a bit of her breasts every time she drew a pint. Red hair she had, well not exactly red, I don't know the word, not so *coarse* as red. My mother said for me to keep off her, my mother is a big Bible woman, though nacherly she couldn't go to chapel down our way being she kept a pub… Well, Monica, this barmaid, she slept in the attic, it's a big 'ouse, the Bute's Arms. And I was nineteen. You can't always answer for yourself, can you? It was my pub by rights, *mine*. She was *my* barmaid. That's how my father'd have said if he wasn't dead. My mother wouldn't have no barmaids when he was alive. Monica knew what she was doing all right. She wanted the pub and the big double bed; she couldn't wait… It didn't seem much to pay for sleeping with a woman like that… Well, then I went back to barracks, and it wasn't till I told my mate and he called me a sucker that I knew I couldn't… Nothing went right after that. She took good care to get pregnant, Monica did, and my mother threw her out. But it was my baby, and I married her without telling my mother. It was *my* affair, wasn't it? *Mine.*'

How long he had been in telling all this Beale couldn't remember. There was nothing to pin that evening upon; the fire and the logs drying beside the fire, the circle of crickets, the sudden blundering of moths into the warm zone of the fire and thoughtful faces, the myopic sleepy stare of fatigue, and those bitter distasteful words within intervals of thought and waiting. Not until now did Beale realize that there had been no hard luck story told, no gambit for sympathy or compassionate leave or a poor person's divorce. But a man talking into a wood fire in the remote asylums of distance, and slowly explaining the twisted and evil curvature of his being.

'She told me she'd get her own back on me for my mother turning her out… And she did… I know a man in my own regiment that slept with her on leave. But the kid is mine. My mother got the kid for me. She shan't spoil the kid. Nobody'll spoil the kid, neither Monica nor me… I can't make it out, how is it a woman is so wonderful, I mean in a bedroom? I should 'a'murdered her, it would be better than this, this hating her all the time. Wouldn't it?…'

'The Tommy cooker's O.K. now, sir,' the driver said. 'The wind was blowing the flame back all the time. O.K. now with this screen. What's it to be? There's only bully left.'

'Eh? What?' Beale said. 'Oh, supper? Bully? I can't eat any more bully. Can't we get some eggs or something? Ten days with bully twice a day is plenty, can you eat bully?'

'Can't say I fancy it,' the driver said. 'I'll go down the road and see if I can get some eggs.'

'I shouldn't bother,' Beale said. 'The storm will get you if you go far. Besides, it's dangerous down the town road. They've been rioting since Gandhi and Nehru were arrested last week. Better brew up and forget about the food.'

Beale was by nature and by his job as a staff officer one who is always doing things and forgetting about them. It was convenient as well as necessary to him. His *Pending* basket was always empty. He never had a load on his mind.

'I'll take a walk just the same,' the driver said. 'Maybe I'll find a chicken laying on the road. I won't be long.'

He was a good scrounger, it was a matter of pride with him to get anything that was wanted, mosquito poles, or water or anything. And every night, whether they were in the forest or the desert plains that encompass Indore, he had announced his intention of walking down the road.

Some impulse caused Beale to delay him a moment.

'Remember,' Beale said, 'the other night, you said you saw the collective farms in Palestine?'

'Aye,' said the driver, standing in the huge deformity of the hunchbacked shadow that the lamp projected from his slovenly head.

'They were good places, those farms?' Beale asked.

'Aye, they were,' the driver said, steadying his childish gaze. 'They didn't have money, they didn't buy and sell. They shared what they had and the doctor and the school teacher the same as the labourer or the children, all the same, all living together. Orange groves they lived in, and I would like to go back there.'

He stepped down from the porch and the enormous shadows vanished from the roof and from the wall. Beale sat on, the biscuit tin of water warming slowly on the cooker, the flying ants casting their wings upon the glass of the lamp and the sheets of his bed. An orange grove in Palestine... He was experiencing one of those enlargements of the imagination that come once or perhaps twice to a man, and recreate him subtly and profoundly. And he was thinking simply this—that some things are possible and other things are impossible to us. Beyond the mass of vivid and sensuous impressions which he had allowed the war to impose upon him were the quiet categories of the possible and the quieter frozen infinities of the impossible. And he must get back to those certainties... The night falls, and the dance bands turn on the heat. The indolent arrive in their taxis, the popsies and the good timers, the lonely good-looking boys and the indifferent erotic women. Swing music sways across the bay from the urbane permissive ballrooms of the Taj and Green's. *In the Mood, It's foolish but it's fun,* some doughboys cracking whips in the coffee room, among apprehensive glances, the taxi drivers buy a betel leaf and spit red saliva over the running board, the panders touch the sleeves of soldiers, the crowd huddles beneath the Gateway, turning up collars and umbrellas everywhere against the thin sane arrows of the rain. And who is she whose song is the world spinning, whose lambent streams cast their curved ways about you and about, whose languors are the infinite desires of the unknowing? Is she the girl behind the grille, in the side street where they play gramophone records and you pay ten chips for a whisky and you suddenly feel a godalmighty yen for whoever it is in your arms? But beyond that, beyond that? Why had he failed with this woman, why had it been impossible with that woman? He collected the swirl of thought and knew that he could not generalize as the driver had done in the glow of the wood fire. Woman. The gardener at the boarding school he went to used to say things about women. Turvey his name was. Turvey, the headmaster called him, but the boys had to say *Mr* Turvey. Mr Turvey didn't hold with mixed bathing, not at any price, because woman wasn't clean like man, he said. And when the boys demurred, thinking of soft pledges and film stars and the moon, Mr Turvey would wrinkle his saturnine face and say, 'Course you young gentlemen knows better than me. I only been married fifteen years. I don't know nothing of course.' And maybe this conversation would be while he was emptying the ordure from the latrines into the oil drum on iron wheels which he trundled each morning down to his sewage pits in the school gardens.

But in an intenser lucidity Beale knew he must not generalize. There would be perhaps one woman out of many, one life out of many, two things possible—if life itself were possible, and if he had not debased himself among the impossibilities by then. The orange grove in Palestine…

And then he realized that the water in the biscuit tin was boiling and he knelt to put the tea and tinned milk into the two enamel mugs. As he knelt a drop of rain the size of a coin pitted his back. And another. And a third. He shuddered. Ten days they'd been on the road, making this reconnaissance for a projected Army exercise, and each day had been nothing but speed and distance hollow in the head, the mileometer ticking up the daily two hundred, the dust of a hundred villages justifying their weariness with its ashes, and tomorrow also only speed and distance and the steadiness of the six cylinders. And he'd been dreaming of a Bombay whore whose red kiss he still had not washed from his arm, allowing her to enter where she would and push into oblivion the few things that were possible to him in the war and the peace. And now the rain made him shudder and he felt all the loneliness of India about him and he knew he had never been more alone. So he was content to watch the storm gather, operating against him from a heavy fulcrum in the east, lashing the bungalow

and the trees, infuriating the night. The cooker spluttered and
went out. He made no move to use the boiling water upon the
tea. The moths flew in from the rain, and the grasshoppers
and the bees. The frogs grunted and creached in the swirling
mud and grass, the night was animate and violent. He waited
without moving until the violence of the storm was spent.
Then he looked at his watch. It was, as he thought. The driver
had been gone an hour and twenty minutes. He knew he must
go and look for him.

He loaded his revolver carefully and buckled on his holster
over his bush shirt. He called for the old caretaker, but there
was no reply. The bungalow was empty. He turned down the
wick of the lamp and putting on his cap, stepped softly into
the night. It was easy to get lost. It would be difficult to find
anything tonight, unless it was plumb in the main road.

His feet felt under the streaming-water for the stones of
the road. The banyan tree he remembered, it was just beyond
the pull-in. Its mass was over him now, he could feel it over
his head. It was going to be difficult. The nearest cantonment
was four hundred miles away; in any case the roads were too
flooded now for him to retrace his way to Mhow. If he went
on to Baroda, Ahmedabad—but the Mahi river would be in
spate also. The lines down everywhere, too. They would have
to go on, that he felt sure about. Before daybreak, too. It wasn't
safe here. If only he could find the driver. He was irritated
with the driver, irritated in a huge cloudy way, for bungling
yet one more thing, for leaving him alone with so much on

his hands, for insisting on looking for eggs. He'd known something would happen.

He felt the driver with his foot and knelt down over him in the swirling road and felt for his heart under his sodden shirt and cursed him in irritation and concern. Dead as a duckboard, knifed. The rain came on again and he tried to lift up the corpse the way he'd been taught, turning it first on to its back and standing firmly astride it. But the driver was obstinate and heavy and for a long time he refused to be lifted up.

He carried the deadweight back up the road, sweating and bitched by the awkward corpse, stumbling and trying in vain to straighten himself. What a bloody mess, he kept saying; I told him not to go and get eggs; did he have to have eggs for supper? It became a struggle between himself and the corpse, who was trying to slide down off his back and stay lying on the road. He had half a mind to let it have its way.

He got back eventually and backed himself against the veranda like a lorry, letting the body slide off his back; the head fell crack against the side wall and he said 'Sorry,' and put a sack between the cheek and the ground. The kid was soaking wet and wet red mud in his hair; he wiped his face up a bit with cotton-waste and put a blanket over him while he packed the kit up and stowed it in the truck. He noticed the tea and sugar in the mugs and tried the temper of the water. It was too cold. He regretted it. He had the truck packed by the end of half an hour, his own bedding roll stretched on top of the baggage ready for the passenger. He hoped he'd be agreeable this time.

He resisted a bit but he had stiffened a little and was more manageable. He backed him into the truck and then climbed in, pulling him on to the blanket by his armpits. Not until he'd put up the tailboard and got him all ready did he feel any ease. He sighed. They were away. He got into the driving seat to switch on the ignition. Then he realized there was no key. He felt a momentary panic. But surely the driver had it. He slipped out and, in the darkness and the drive of the rain, searched in the man's pockets. Paybook, matches, identity discs (must remember that, didn't even know his name), at last the keys.

He started the engine and let her warm up, slipped her into second and drove slowly out. The old caretaker never appeared, and Beale wondered whether he should say anything of his suspicions regarding the old man when he made his report. Unfortunately, there was no evidence. Still, they were away from there; he sighed with relief as the compulsion under which he had been acting relaxed. He had this extra sense, of which he was proud, of being able to feel the imminence of danger as others feel a change in the weather; it didn't help him in Libya, perhaps it hindered him there; but in a pub in Durban it had got him out in the nick of time; he'd edged for the door before a shot was fired. He knew tonight all right. The moment he saw that dull red lever of storm raised over his head, and the old caretaker had shrugged his shoulders after his warning had been laughed off. You had to bluff them; only sometimes bluff wasn't enough and then you had to get away, face or no face. Now he tried to remember the route on the map; driving blind, the best thing was to go slow and pull in somewhere a few miles on. Maybe the sun would rise sometime and he could dry out the map and work out the best route; no more native towns for him; he wanted to get to a cantonment if possible. Otherwise he'd look for the police lines at Dohad or Jabhua or wherever the next place was. But every time he thought of pulling in, a disinclination to stop the engine made him keep his drenched ammunition boot on the accelerator pedal. When he came to a road junction he followed his fancy; there is such a thing as letting the car do the guiding.

He drove for six hours before the night stirred at all. Then his red-veined eyes felt the slight lessening in the effectiveness of the headlights that presaged the day. When he could see the red berm of the road and the flooded paddy-fields lapping the bank, he at last pulled up under a tree and composed himself over the wheel, placing his cheek against the rim, avoiding the horn at the centre. He fell at once into a stiff rigid sleep.

A tribe of straggling gipsies passed him soon after dawn. They made no sound, leading their mules and camels along the soft berm on the other side of the road, mixing their own ways with no other's. The sun lay back of the blue rain-clouds, making the earth steam. The toads hopped out of the mud and rested under the stationary truck. Land-crabs came out of the earth and sat on the edge of their holes. Otherwise no one passed. The earth seemed content to let him have his sleep out. He woke about noon, touched by the sun as it passed.

He felt guilty. Guilty of neglect of duty, having slept at his post? Then he got a grip on himself and rationalized the dreadful guilt away. What could he have done about it? The driver had been murdered. What did they expect him to do? Stay there and give them a second treat? Stay there and investigate? Or get on and report it. Why hadn't he reported it earlier? How could he? The lines were down, the roads flooded behind him, he was trying his best; he couldn't help sleeping for a couple of hours. Yet the guilt complex persisted. It was bad dream and he had some evil in him, a soft lump of evil in his brain. But why? If he'd told the man to go for eggs it would be different. He was bound to be all right as long as he had his facts right. Was there an accident report to be filled in immediately, in duplicate, Army Form B- something-or-other? He took out his notebook, but the paper was too wet to take his hard pencil. 2300 hrs. on 23 August 1942 deceased stated his desire to get some eggs. I warned him that disturbances of a political character had occurred in the area… He shook himself, bleary and sore-throated, in his musty overalls, and thought a shave and some food would put him right. He went round to the back of the truck. The body had slipped with the jolting of the road. He climbed in and looked at the ashen face. The eyes were closed, the face had sunk into an expressionless inanition, it made him feel indifferent to the whole thing. Poor sod. Where was his hate now? Was he grieving that the woman, Mona was it, would get a pension out of him now? Did he still hate her? He seemed to have let the whole matter drop. Death was something without hate in it. But he didn't want to do anything himself except shave and eat and get the whole thing buttoned up. He tore himself away from the closed soiled face and ferreted about for his shaving kit. He found it at last, and after shaving in the muddy rain water he ate a few hard biscuits and stuffed a few more into his pocket. Then he lashed the canvas down over the tailboard and got back to the wheel. The truck was slow to start. The bonnet had been leaking and the plugs were wet in the cylinder heads. She wouldn't spark for a minute or two. Anxiety swept over him. He cursed the truck viciously. Then she sparked on a couple of cylinders, stuttered for a minute as the others dried out, and settled down steadily. He ran her away carefully and again relaxed. He was dead scared of being stranded with the body. There wasn't even a shovel on the truck.

After driving for an hour he realized he didn't know where he was. He was in the centre of a vast plain of paddy-fields, lined by raised bunds and hedged with cactus along the road. White herons and tall fantastic cranes stood by the pools in the hollows. He pulled up to try and work out his position. But his map was nowhere to be found. He must have left it at the dak bungalow in his haste. He looked at his watch; it had stopped. Something caved in inside him, a sensation of panic, of an enemy against whose machinations he had failed to take the most elementary precautions. He was lost.

He moved on again at once. There was distance. The mile-ometer still measured something? By sunset he would do so many miles. How much of the day was left? Without the sun how could he tell? He was panicky at not knowing these things; he scarcely knew more than the man in the back of the truck. So he drove on and on, passing nobody but a tribe of gipsies with their mules and camels, and dark peasants driving their bullocks knee-deep in the alluvial mud before their simple wooden ploughs. He drove as fast as the track would allow; in some places it was flooded and narrow, descending to narrow causeways swept by brown streams which he only just managed to cross. He drove till the land was green with evening, and in the crepuscular uncertainty he halted and decided to kip down for the night. He would need petrol; it was kept in tins in the back of the truck; it meant pulling the body out, or making him sit away in a corner. He didn't want to disturb the kid. He'd been jolted all day; and now this indignity. He did all he had to do with a humility that was alien to him. Respect he knew; but this was more than respect; obedience and necessity he knew, but this was more than either of these. It was somehow an admission of the integrity of the man, a new interest in what he was and what he had left behind. He got some soap and a towel, after filling his tanks, and when he had washed himself he propped the driver up against the tailboard and sponged him clean and put P.T. shoes on his feet instead of the boots that had so swollen his feet. When he had laid him out on the blankets and covered him with a sheet, he rested from his exertions, and as he recovered his breath he glanced covertly at him, satisfied that he had done something for him. What would the woman have done, Monica? Would she have flirted with him? Most women did, and he didn't discourage them. But this woman, my God, he'd bloody well beat her up. It was her doing, this miserable end, this mess-up. He hadn't gone down the road to get eggs; he'd gone to get away from her. It must have been a habit of his, at nights, to compose himself. She'd bitched it all. He could just see her. And she still didn't know a thing about him, not the first thing. Yes, he hated her all right, the voluptuous bitch.

He slept at the wheel again, falling asleep with a biscuit still half chewed in his mouth. He had erotic dreams, this woman Monica drawing him a pint, and her mouth and her breasts and the shallow taunting eyes; and the lights in her attic bedroom with the door ajar, and the wooden stairs creaking. And the dawn then laid its grey fingers upon him and he woke with the same feeling of guilt and shame, a grovelling debased mood, that had seized him the first morning. He got up, stretching himself, heady with vertigo and phlegm, and washed himself in the paddy flood. He went round to the back of the truck to get some biscuits. He got them quietly, the boy was still sleeping, and he said to himself that he would get him through today, honest he would. He had to.

The sun came out and the sky showed a young summer blue. The trees wakened and shook soft showers of rain off their leaves. Hills showed blue as lavender and when he came to the crossroads he steered north-west by the sun, reckoning to make the coast road somewhere near Baroda. There would be a cantonment not far from there, and a Service dump for coffins, and someone to whom he could make a report. It would be an immense relief. His spirits rose. Driving was tricky; the worn treads of the tyres tended to skid, the road wound up and down the ghats, through tall loose scrub; but he did not miss seeing the shy jungle wanderers moving through the bush with their bows, tall lithe men like fauns with black hair over their eyes that were like grapes. They would stand a moment under a tree, and glide away back into the bush. There were villages now, and women of light olive skin beating their saris on the stones, rhythmically, and their breasts uncovered.

And then, just when he felt he was out of the lost zones, in the late afternoon, he came down a long sandy track through cactus to a deep and wide river at which the road ended. A gipsy tribe was fording it and he watched them to gauge the depth of the river. The little mules, demure as mice, kicked up against the current, nostrils too near the water to neigh; the camels followed the halter, stately as bishops, picking their calm way. The babies sat on their parents' heads, the women unwound their saris and put them in a bundle on their crowns, the water touched their breasts. And Beale pushed his truck into bottom gear and nosed her cautiously into the stream. Midway across the brown tide swept up to his sparking plugs and the engine stopped. He knew at once that he was done for. The river came up in waves over the sideboards and his whole concern was that the boy inside would be getting wet. A gipsy waded past impersonally, leading two bright-eyed grey mules. Beale hailed him. He nodded and went on. Beale called out 'Help!', the gipsies gathered on the far bank and discussed it. He waved and eventually three of them came wading out to him. He knew he must abandon the truck till a recovery section could be sent out to salvage it, but he must take his companion with him, naturally. When the gipsies reached him he pointed to the back of the truck, unlaced the tarpaulin and showed them the corpse. They nodded their heads gravely. Their faces were serious and hard. He contrived to show them what he wanted and when he climbed in they helped him intelligently to hoist the body out. They contrived to get it onto their heads, ducking down under the tailboard till their faces were submerged in the scum of the flood.

They carried him ashore that way, Beale following with his revolver and webbing. They held a conclave on the sand while the women wrung out their saris and the children crowded about the body. Beale stood in the centre of these lean outlandish men, not understanding a word. They talked excitedly, abruptly, looking at him and at the corpse. He fished his wallet out of his pocket and showed them a five-rupee note. He pointed to the track and to the mules. They nodded and came to some domestic agreement. One of them led a little mule down to the stream and they strapped a board across its bony moulting back, covering the board with sacking. Four of them lifted the body up and lashed it along the spar. Then they smiled at Beale, obviously asking for his approval of their skill. He nodded back and said 'That's fine'. The gipsies laid their panniers on the mules, the women wound their saris about their swarthy bodies, called their children, formed behind their men. The muleteer grinned and nodded his head to Beale. The caravanserai went forward across the sands. Beale turned back once to look at the truck, but he was too bloody tired and fed up to mind. It would stay there; it was settled in; if the floods rose it would disappear; if they fell so much the better. He couldn't help making a balls of it all. He had the body, that was one proof; they could find the truck if they came to look for it, that was the second proof. If they wanted an accident report they could wait. If they thought he was puddled they could sack him when they liked. What was it all about, anyway?

Stumbling up the track in the half-light among the ragged garish gipsies he gradually lost the stiff self-consciousness with which he had first approached them. He was thinking of a page near the beginning of a history book he had studied in the Sixth at school in 1939. About the barbarian migrations in pre-history; the Celts and Iberians, Goths and Vandals and Huns. Once Life had been nothing worth recording beyond the movements of people like these, camels and asses piled with the poor property of their days, panniers, rags, rope, gramm and dahl, lambs and kids too new to walk, barefooted, long-haired people rank with sweat, animals shivering with ticks, old women striving to keep up with the rest of the family. He kept away from the labouring old women, preferring the tall girls who walked under the primitive smooth heads of the camels. He kept his eye on the corpse, but he seemed comfortable enough. Except he was beginning to corrupt. There was a faint whiff of badness about him... What did the gipsies do? They would burn him, perhaps, if the journey took too long. How many days to Baroda? The muleteer nodded his head and grinned.

Well, as long as he had the man's identity discs and paybook, he would be covered. He must have those... He slipped the identity discs over the wet blue head and matted hair and put them in his overall pocket. He would be alright now, even if they burned him... It would be a bigger fire than the one they had sat by and fed with twigs and talked about women together that night, how many nights ago?

He wished, though, that he knew where they were going. They only smiled and nodded when he asked. Maybe they weren't going anywhere much, except perhaps to some pasture, to some well.

A PIECE OF CAKE

Roald Dahl (1916–1990)

Born mid-way through the First World War to Norwegian parents settled in Wales, Dahl was travelling in Africa when the Second World War broke out. He volunteered in the Royal Air Force in Kenya, where he also received his flying training. In 1940, serving in the Western Desert, Dahl crashed when his plane ran out of fuel, sustaining life-changing injuries. He subsequently served in the Mediterranean before being invalided home to Britain at last and working in a security post. A by-product of Dahl's crash landing was his breaking into print, as he was asked to write an account of his experiences for the popular American weekly, the *Saturday Evening Post*.

I DO NOT REMEMBER MUCH OF IT; NOT BEFOREHAND anyway; not until it happened.

There was the landing at Fouka, where the Blenheim boys were helpful and gave us tea while we were being refuelled. I remember the quietness of the Blenheim boys, how they came into the mess-tent to get some tea and sat down to drink it without saying anything; how they got up and went out when they had finished drinking and still they did not say anything. And I knew that each one was holding himself together because the going was not very good right then. They were having to go out too often, and there were no replacements coming along.

We thanked them for the tea and went out to see if they had finished refuelling our Gladiators. I remember that there was a wind blowing which made the wind-sock stand out straight, like a signpost, and the sand was blowing up around our legs and making a rustling noise as it swished against the tents, and the tents flapped in the wind so that they were like canvas men clapping their hands.

'Bomber boys unhappy,' Peter said.

'Not unhappy,' I answered.

'Well, they're browned off.'

'No. They've had it, that's all. But they'll keep going. You can see they're trying to keep going.'

Our two old Gladiators were standing beside each other in the sand and the airmen in their khaki shirts and shorts seemed still to be busy with the refuelling. I was wearing a thin white cotton flying suit and Peter had on a blue one. It wasn't necessary to fly with anything warmer.

Peter said, 'How far away is it?'

'Twenty-one miles beyond Charing Cross,' I answered, 'on the right side of the road.' Charing Cross was where the desert road branched north to Mersah Matruh. The Italian army was outside Mersah, and they were doing pretty well. It was about the only time, so far as I know, that the Italians have done pretty well. Their morale goes up and down like a sensitive altimeter, and right then it was at forty thousand because the Axis was on top of the world. We hung around waiting for the refuelling to finish.

Peter said, 'It's a piece of cake.'

'Yes. It ought to be easy.'

We separated and I climbed into my cockpit. I have always remembered the face of the airman who helped me to strap in. He was oldish, about forty, and bald except for a neat patch of golden hair at the back of his head. His face was all wrinkles, his eyes were like my grandmother's eyes, and he looked as though he had spent his life helping to strap in pilots who never came back. He stood on the wing pulling my straps and said, 'Be careful. There isn't any sense not being careful.'

'Piece of cake,' I said.

'Like hell.'

'Really. It isn't anything at all. It's a piece of cake.'

I don't remember much about the next bit; I only remember about later on. I suppose we took off from Fouka and flew west towards Mersah, and I suppose we flew at about eight hundred feet. I suppose we saw the sea to starboard, and I suppose— no, I am certain—that it was blue and that it was beautiful, especially where it rolled up on to the sand and made a long thick white line east and west as far as you could see. I suppose we flew over Charing Cross and flew on for twenty-one miles to where they had said it would be, but I do not know. I know only that there was trouble, lots and lots of trouble, and I know that we had turned round and were coming back when the trouble got worse. The biggest trouble of all was that I was too low to bale out, and it is from that point on that my memory comes back to me. I remember the dipping of the nose of the aircraft and I remember looking down the nose of the machine at the ground and seeing a little clump of camel-thorn growing there all by itself. I remember seeing some rocks lying in the sand beside the camel-thorn, and the camel-thorn and the sand and the rocks leapt out of the ground and came to me. I remember that very clearly.

Then there was a small gap of not-remembering. It might have been one second or it might have been thirty; I do not know. I have an idea that it was very short, a second perhaps, and next I heard a *crumph* on the right as the starboard wing tank caught fire, then another *crumph* on the left as the port tank did the same. To me that was not significant, and for a while I sat still, feeling comfortable, but a little drowsy. I couldn't see with my eyes, but that was not significant either. There was nothing to worry about. Nothing at all. Not until I felt the hotness around my legs. At first it was only a warmness and that was all right too, but all at once it was a hotness, a very stinging scorching hotness up and down the sides of each leg.

I knew that the hotness was unpleasant, but that was all I knew. I disliked it, so I curled my legs up under the seat and waited. I think there was something wrong with the telegraph system between the body and the brain. It did not seem to be working very well. Somehow it was a bit slow in telling the brain all about it and in asking for instructions. But I believe a message eventually got through, saying, 'Down here there is a great hotness. What shall we do? (Signed) Left Leg and Right Leg.' For a long time there was no reply. The brain was figuring the matter out.

Then slowly, word by word, the answer was tapped over the wires. 'The—plane—is—burning. Get—out—repeat—get—out—get—out.' The order was relayed to the whole system, to all the muscles in the legs, arms and body, and the muscles went to work. They tried their best; they pushed a little and pulled a little, and they strained greatly, but it wasn't any good. Up went another telegram, 'Can't get out. Something holding us in.' The answer to this one took even longer in arriving, so I just sat there waiting for it to come, and all the time the hotness increased. Something was holding me down and it was up to the brain to find out what it was. Was it giants' hands pressing on my shoulders, or heavy stones or houses or steam rollers or filing cabinets or gravity or was it ropes? Wait a minute. Ropes—ropes. The message was beginning to come through. It came very slowly. 'Your—straps. Undo—your—straps.' My arms received the message and went to work. They tugged at the straps, but they wouldn't undo. They tugged again and again, a little feebly, but as hard as they could, and it wasn't any use. Back went the message, 'How do we undo the straps?'

This time I think that I sat there for three or four minutes waiting for the answer. It wasn't any use hurrying or getting impatient. That was the one thing of which I was sure. But what a long time it was all taking. I said aloud, 'Bugger it. I'm going to be burnt. I'm...' but I was interrupted. The answer was coming—no, it wasn't—yes, it was, it was slowly coming through. 'Pull—out—the—quick—release—pin—you—bloody—fool—and—hurry.'

Out came the pin and the straps were loosed. Now, let's get out. Let's get out, let's get out. But I couldn't do it. I simply lift myself out of the cockpit. Arms and legs tried their best but it wasn't any use. A last desperate message was flashed upwards and this time it was marked 'Urgent'.

'Something else is holding us down,' it said. 'Something else, something else, something heavy.'

Still the arms and legs did not fight. They seemed to know instinctively that there was no point in using up their strength. They stayed quiet and waited for the answer, and oh what a time it took. Twenty, thirty, forty hot seconds. None of them really white hot yet, no sizzling of flesh or smell of burning meat, but that would come any moment now, because those old Gladiators aren't made of stressed steel like a Hurricane or a Spit. They have taut canvas wings, covered with magnificently inflammable dope, and underneath there are hundreds of small thin sticks, the kind you put under the logs for kindling, only these are drier and thinner. If a clever man said, 'I am going to build a big thing that will burn better and quicker than anything else in the world,' and if he applied himself diligently to his task, he would probably finish up by building something very like a Gladiator. I sat still waiting.

Then suddenly the reply, beautiful in its briefness, but at the same time explaining everything. 'Your—parachute—turn—the—buckle.'

I turned the buckle, released the parachute harness and with some effort hoisted myself up and tumbled over the side of the cockpit. Something seemed to be burning, so I rolled about a bit in the sand, then crawled away from the fire on all fours and lay down.

I heard some of my machine-gun ammunition going off in the heat and I heard some of the bullets thumping into the sand near by. I did not worry about them; I merely heard them.

Things were beginning to hurt. My face hurt most. There was something wrong with my face. Something had happened to it. Slowly I put up a hand to feel it. It was sticky. My nose didn't seem to be there. I tried to feel my teeth, but I cannot remember whether I came to any conclusion about them. I think I dozed off.

All of a sudden there was Peter. I heard his voice and I heard him dancing around and yelling like a madman and shaking my hand and saying, 'Jesus, I thought you were still inside. I came down half a mile away and ran like hell. Are you all right?'

I said, 'Peter, what has happened to my nose?'

I heard him striking a match in the dark: The night comes quickly in the desert. There was a pause.

'It actually doesn't seem to be there very much,' he said. 'Does it hurt?'

'Don't be a bloody fool, of course it hurts.'

He said he was going back to his machine to get some morphia out of his emergency pack, but he came back again soon, saying he couldn't find his aircraft in the dark.

'Peter,' I said, 'I can't see anything.'

'It's night,' he answered. 'I can't see either.'

It was cold now. It was bitter cold, and Peter lay down close alongside so that we could both keep a little warmer. Every now and then he would say, 'I've never seen a man without a nose before.' I kept spewing a lot of blood and every time

I did it, Peter lit a match. Once he gave me a cigarette, but it got wet and I didn't want it anyway.

I do not know how long we stayed there and I remember only very little more. I remember that I kept telling Peter that there was a tin of sore-throat tablets in my pocket, and that he should take one, otherwise he would catch my sore throat. I remember asking him where we were and him saying, 'We're between the two armies,' and then I remember English voices from an English patrol asking if we were Italians. Peter said something to them; I cannot remember what he said.

Later I remember hot thick soup and one spoonful making me sick. And all the time the pleasant feeling that Peter was around, being wonderful, doing wonderful things and never going away. That is all that I can remember.

The men stood beside the airplane painting away and talking about the heat.

'Painting pictures on the aircraft,' I said.

'Yes,' said Peter. 'It's a great idea. It's subtle.'

'Why?' I said. 'Just you tell me.'

'They're funny pictures,' he said. 'The German pilots will all laugh when they see them; they'll shake so with their laughing that they won't be able to shoot straight.'

'Oh baloney baloney baloney.'

'No, it's a great idea. It's fine. Come and have a look.'

We ran towards the line of aircraft. 'Hop, skip, jump,' said Peter. 'Hop skip jump, keep in time.'

'Hop skip jump,' I said, 'Hop skip jump,' and we danced along.

The painter on the first aeroplane had a straw hat on his head and a sad face. He was copying the drawing out of a magazine, and when Peter saw it he said, 'Boy oh boy look at that picture,' and he began to laugh. His laugh began with a rumble and grew quickly into a belly-roar and he slapped his thighs with his hands both at the same time and went on laughing with his body doubled up and his mouth wide open and his eyes shut. His silk top hat fell off his head on to the sand.

'That's not funny,' I said.

'Not funny!' he cried. 'What d'you mean "not funny"? Look at me. Look at me laughing. Laughing like this I couldn't hit anything. I couldn't hit a hay wagon or a house or a louse.' And he capered about on the sand, gurgling and shaking with laughter. Then he seized me by the arm and we danced over to the next aeroplane. 'Hop skip jump,' he said. 'Hop skip jump.'

There was a small man with a crumpled face writing a long story on the fuselage with a red crayon. His straw hat was perched right on the back of his head and his face was shiny with sweat.

'Good morning,' he said. 'Good morning, good morning,' and he swept his hat off his head in a very elegant way.

Peter said, 'Shut up,' and bent down and began to read what the little man had been writing. All the time Peter was spluttering and rumbling with laughter, and as he read he began to laugh afresh. He rocked from one side to the other and danced around on the sand slapping his thighs with his hands and bending his body. 'Oh my, what a story, what a story, what a story. Look at me. Look at me laughing,' and he hopped about on his toes, shaking his head and chortling like a madman. Then suddenly I saw the joke and I began to laugh with him. I laughed so much that my stomach hurt and I fell down and rolled around on the sand and roared and roared because it was so funny that there was nothing else I could do.

'Peter, you're marvellous,' I shouted. 'But can all those German pilots read English?'

'Oh hell,' he said. 'Oh hell. Stop,' he shouted. 'Stop your work,' and the painters all stopped their painting and turned round slowly and looked at Peter. They did a little caper on their toes and began to chant in unison. 'Rubbishy things—on all the wings, on all the wings, on all the wings,' they chanted.

'Shut up,' said Peter. 'We're in a jam. We must keep calm. Where's my top hat?'

'What?' I said.

'You can speak German,' he said. 'You must translate for us. He will translate for you,' he shouted to the painters. 'He will translate.'

Then I saw his black top hat lying in the sand. I looked away, then I looked around and saw it again. It was a silk opera-hat and it was lying there on its side in the sand.

'You're mad,' I shouted. 'You're madder than hell. You don't know what you're doing. You'll get us all killed. You're absolutely plumb crazy, do you know that? You're crazier than hell. My God, you're crazy.'

'Goodness, what a noise you're making. You mustn't shout like that; it's not good for you.' This was a woman's voice. 'You've made yourself all hot,' she said, and I felt someone wiping my forehead with a handkerchief. 'You mustn't work yourself up like that.'

Then she was gone and I saw only the sky, which was pale blue. There were no clouds and all around were the German fighters. They were above, below and on every side and there was no way I could go; there was nothing I could do. They took it in turns to come in to attack and they flew their aircraft carelessly, banking and looping and dancing in the air. But I was not frightened, because of the funny pictures on my wings. I was confident and I thought, 'I am going to fight a hundred of them alone and I'll shoot them all down. I'll shoot them while they are laughing; that's what I'll do.'

Then they flew closer. The whole sky was full of them. There were so many that I did not know which ones to watch and which ones to attack. There were so many that they made a black curtain over the sky and only here and there could I see a little of the blue showing through. But there was enough to patch a Dutchman's trousers, which was all that mattered. So long as there was enough to do that, then everything was all right.

Still they flew closer. They came nearer and nearer, right up in front of my face so that I saw only the black crosses which stood out brightly against the colour of the Messerschmitts and against the blue of the sky; and as I turned my head quickly from one side to the other I saw more aircraft and more crosses and then I saw nothing but the arms of the crosses and the blue of the sky. The arms had hands and they joined together and made a circle and danced around my Gladiator, while the engines of the Messerschmitts sang joyfully in a deep voice. They were playing Oranges and Lemons and every now and then two would detach themselves and come out into the middle of the floor and make an attack and I knew then that it was Oranges and Lemons. They banked and swerved and danced upon their toes and they leant against the air first to one side, then to the other. 'Oranges and Lemons said the bells of St. Clements,' sang the engines.

But I was still confident. I could dance better than they and I had a better partner. She was the most beautiful girl in the world. I looked down and saw the curve of her neck and the gentle slope of her pale shoulders and I saw her slender arms, eager and outstretched.

Suddenly I saw some bullet holes in my starboard wing and I got angry and scared both at the same time; but mostly I got angry. Then I got confident and I said, 'The German who did that had no sense of humour. There's always one man in a party who has no sense of humour. But there's nothing to worry about; there's nothing at all to worry about.'

Then I saw more bullet holes and I got scared. I slid back the hood of the cockpit and stood up and shouted, 'You fools, look at the funny pictures. Look at the one on my tail; look at the story on my fuselage. Please look at the story on my fuselage.'

But they kept on coming. They tripped into the middle of the floor in twos, shooting at me as they came. And the engines of the Messerschmitts sang loudly. 'When will you pay me, said the bells of Old Bailey?' sang the engines, and as they sang the black crosses danced and swayed to the rhythm of the music. There were more holes in my wings, in the engine cowling and in the cockpit.

Then suddenly there were some in my body.

But there was no pain, even when I went into a spin, when the wings of my plane went flip, flip, flip, flip, faster and faster, when the blue sky and the black sea chased each other round and round until there was no longer any sky or sea but just the flashing of the sun as I turned. But the black crosses were following me down, still dancing and still holding hands and I could still hear the singing of their engines. 'Here comes a candle to light you to bed, here comes a chopper to chop off your head,' sang the engines.

Still the wings went flip flip, flip flip, and there was neither sky nor sea around me, but only the sun.

Then there was only the sea. I could see it below me and I could see the white horses, and I said to myself, 'Those are white horses riding a rough sea.' I knew then that my brain was going well because of the white horses and because of the sea. I knew that there was not much time because the sea and the white horses were nearer, the white horses were bigger and the sea was like a sea and like water, not like a smooth plate. Then there was only one white horse, rushing forward madly with his bit in his teeth, foaming at the mouth, scattering the spray with his hooves and arching his neck as he ran. He galloped on madly over the sea, riderless and uncontrollable, and I could tell that we were going to crash.

After that it was warmer, and there were no black crosses and there was no sky. But it was only warm because it was not hot and it was not cold. I was sitting in a great red chair made of velvet and it was evening. There was a wind blowing from behind.

'Where am I?' I said.

'You are missing. You are missing, believed killed.'

'Then I must tell my mother.'

'You can't. You can't use that phone.'

'Why not?'

'It goes only to God.'

'What did you say I was?'

'Missing, believed killed.'

'That's not true. It's a lie. It's a lousy lie because here I am and I'm not missing. You're just trying to frighten me and you won't succeed. You won't succeed, I tell you, because I know it's a lie and I'm going back to my squadron. You can't stop me because I'll just go. I'm going, you see, I'm going.'

I got up from the red chair and began to run.

'Let me see those X-rays again, nurse.'

'They're here, doctor.' This was the woman's voice again, and now it came closer. 'You have been making a noise tonight, haven't you? Let me straighten your pillow for you, you're pushing it on to the floor.' The voice was close and it was very soft and nice.

'Am I missing?'

'No, of course not. You're fine.'

'They said I was missing.'

'Don't be silly; you're fine.'

Oh everyone's silly, silly, silly, but it was a lovely day, and I did not want to run but I couldn't stop. I kept on running across the grass and I couldn't stop because my legs were carrying me and I had no control over them. It was as if they did not belong to me, although when I looked down I saw that they were mine, that the shoes on the feet were mine and that the legs were joined to my body. But they would not do what I wanted; they just went on running across the field and I had to go with them. I ran and ran and ran, and although in some places the field was rough and bumpy, I never stumbled. I ran past trees and hedges and in one field there were some sheep which stopped their eating and scampered off as I ran past them. Once I saw my mother in a pale grey dress bending down picking mushrooms, and as I ran past she looked up and said, 'My basket's nearly full; shall we go home soon?' but my legs wouldn't stop and I had to go on.

Then I saw the cliff ahead and I saw how dark it was beyond the cliff. There was this great cliff and beyond it there was nothing but darkness, although the sun was shining in the field where I was running. The light of the sun stopped dead at the edge of the cliff and there was only darkness beyond. 'That must be where the night begins,' I thought, and once more I tried to stop but it was not any good. My legs began to go faster towards the cliff and they began to take longer strides, and I reached down with my hand and tried to stop them by clutching the cloth of my trousers, but it did not work; then I tried to fall down. But my legs were nimble, and each time I threw myself I landed on my toes and went on running.

Now the cliff and the darkness were much nearer and I could see that unless I stopped quickly I should go over the edge. Once more I tried to throw myself to the ground and once more I landed on my toes and went on running.

I was going fast as I came to the edge and I went straight on over it into the darkness and began to fall.

At first it was not quite dark. I could see little trees growing out of the face of the cliff, and I grabbed at them with my hands as I went down. Several times I managed to catch hold of a branch, but it always broke off at once because I was so heavy and because I was falling so fast, and once I caught a thick branch with both hands and the tree leaned forward and I heard the snapping of the roots one by one until it came away from the cliff and I went on falling. Then it became darker because the sun and the day were in the fields far away at the top of the cliff, and as I fell I kept my eyes open and watched the darkness turn from grey-black to black, from black to jet black and from jet black to pure liquid blackness which I could touch with my hands but which I could not see. But I went on falling, and it was so black that there was nothing anywhere and it was not any use doing anything or caring or thinking because of the blackness and because of the falling. It was not any use.

'You're better this morning. You're much better.' It was the woman's voice again.

'Hallo.'

'Hallo; we thought you were never going to get conscious.'

'Where am I?'

'In Alexandria; in hospital!'

'How long have I been here?'

'Four days.'

'What time is it?'

'Seven o'clock in the morning.'

'Why can't I see?'

I heard her walking a little closer.

'Oh, we've just put a bandage around your eyes for a bit.'

'How long for?'

'Just for a while. Don't worry. You're fine. You were very lucky, you know.'

I was feeling my face with my fingers but I couldn't feel it; I could only feel something else.

'What's wrong with my face?'

I heard her coming up to the side of my bed and I felt her hand touching my shoulder.

'You mustn't talk any more. You're not allowed to talk. It's bad for you. Just lie still and don't worry. You're fine.'

I heard the sound of her footsteps as she walked across the floor and I heard her open the door and shut it again.

'Nurse,' I said. 'Nurse.'

But she was gone.

THE DISINHERITED

H. E. Bates (1905–1974)

Bates, best known for *The Darling Buds of May* (1958), started his writing career as a reporter for the *Northampton Chronicle* and as a contributor of poetry and a weekly column for the *Kettering Reminder*. His first novel, *The Two Sisters*, was published in 1926. Besides novels, he wrote and published many short stories, which appeared in papers such as the *New Statesman* and the *Manchester Guardian* among others. During the Second World War, the Royal Air Force recruited Bates—by that point a successful professional writer—to work in their public relations department and write morale-boosting fiction about the lives of airmen and women. Writing under the pseudonym 'Flying Officer X', his stories of air force life were enormously successful and were, following publication in magazines during the war, collected as *The Stories of Flying Officer X* (1952).

ON THAT STATION WE HAD PILOTS FROM ALL OVER THE world, so that the sound of the mess, as someone said, was like a Russian bazaar. They came from Holland and Poland, Belgium and Czechoslovakia, France and Norway. We had many French and they had with them brown and yellow men from the Colonial Empire who at dispersal on warm spring afternoons played strange games with pennies in the dry, white dust on the edge of the perimeter. We had many Canadians and New Zealanders, Australians and Africans. There was a West Indian boy, the colour of milky coffee, who was a barrister, and a Lithuanian who played international football. There was a man from Indo-China and another from Tahiti. There was an American and a Swiss and there were negroes, very black and curly, among the ground crews. We had men who had done everything and been everywhere, who had had everything and had lost it all. They had escaped across frontiers and over mountains and down the river valleys of Central Europe; they had come through Libya and Iran and Turkey and round the Cape; they had come through Spain and Portugal or nailed under the planks of little ships wherever a little ship could put safely to sea. They had things in common with themselves that men had nowhere else on earth, and you saw on their faces sometimes a look of sombre silence that could only have been the expression of recollected hatred. But among them all there was only one who had something which no one else had, and he was Capek the Czech. Capek had white hair.

Capek was a night-fighter pilot, so that mostly in the day-time you would find him in the hut at dispersal. The hut was very pleasant and there was a walnut piano and a radio and a miniature billiard-table and easy chairs that had been presented by the mayor of the local town. No one ever played the piano but it was charming all the same. On the walls there were pictures, some in colour, of girls in their underwear and without underwear at all, and rude remarks about pilots who forgot to check their guns. Pilots who had been flying at night lay on the camp beds, sleeping a little, their eyes puffed, using their flying jackets as pillows; or they played cards and groused and talked shop among themselves. They were bored because they were flying too much. They argued about the merits of a four-cannon job as opposed to those of a single gun that fired through the air-screw. They argued about the climate of New Zealand, if it could be compared with the climate of England. They were restless and temperamental, as fighter pilots are apt to be, and it seemed always as if they would have been happier doing anything but the things they were.

Capek alone did not do these things. He did not seem bored or irritable, or tired or temperamental. He did not play billiards and he did not seem interested in the bodies of the girls on the walls. He was never asleep on the beds. He never played cards or argued about the merits of this or that. It seemed sometimes as if he did not belong to us. He sat apart from us, and with his white hair, cultured brown face, clean fine lips and the dark spectacles he wore sometimes against the bright spring sunlight he looked something like a middle-aged provincial professor who had come to take a cure at a health resort in the sun. Seeing him in the street, the bus, the train or the tram, you would never have guessed that he could fly. You would never have guessed that in order to be one of us, to fly with us and fight with us, Capek had come half across the world.

There was a time when a very distinguished personage came to the station and, seeing Capek, asked how long he had been in the Air Force and Capek replied 'Please, seventeen years.' This took his flying life far back beyond the beginning of the war we were fighting; back to the years when some of us were hardly born and when Czechoslovakia had become born again as a nation. Capek had remained in the Air Force all those years, flying heaven knows what types of plane, and becoming finally part of the forces that crumbled away and disintegrated and disappeared under the progress of the tanks that entered Prague in the summer of 1939. Against this progress Capek was one of those who disappeared. He disappeared in a lorry with many others and they rode eastward towards Poland, always retreating and not knowing where they were going.

With Capek was a man named Machakek, and as the retreat went on Capek and Machakek became friends.

Capek and Machakek stayed in Poland all that summer, until the chaos of September. It is not easy to know what Capek and Machakek did; if they were interned, or how, or where, because Capek's English is composed of small difficult words and long difficult silences, often broken only by smiles. 'All time is retreat. Then war start. Poland is in war. Then Germany is coming one way and Russia is coming another.' In this way Capek and Machakek had no escape. They could go neither east nor west. It was too late to go south, and in the north Gdynia had gone. And in time, as Germany moved eastward and Russia westward, Capek and Machakek were taken by the Russians. Capek went to a concentration camp, and Machakek worked in the mines. As prisoners they had a status not easy to define. Russia was not then in the war and Czechoslovakia, politically, did not exist. It seemed in these days as if Russia might come into the war against us. It was very confused and during the period of clarification, if you could call it that, Capek and Machakek went on working in the concentration camp and the mine. 'We remain,' Capek said, 'one year and three quarter.'

Then the war clarified and finally Capek was out of the concentration camp and Machakek was out of the mine. They were together again, still friends, and they moved south, to the Black Sea. Standing on the perimeter track, in the bright spring sun, wearing his dark spectacles, Capek had so little to say about this that he looked exactly like a blind man who has arrived somewhere, after a long time, but for whom the journey is darkness. 'From Black Sea I go to Turkey. Turkey then to Syria. Then Cairo. Then Aden.'

'And Machakek with you?'

'Machakek with me, yes. But only to Aden. After Aden Machakek is going to Bombay on one boat. I am going to Cape Town on other.'

'So Machakek went to India?'

'To India, yes. Is very long way. Is very long time.'

'And you—Cape Town?'

'Yes, me, Cape Town. Then Gibraltar. Then here, England.'

'And Machakek?'

'Machakek is here too. We are both post here. To this squadron.'

The silence that followed this had nothing to do with the past; it had much to do with the present; more to do with Machakek. Through the retreat and the mine and the concentration camp, through the journey to Turkey and Cairo and Aden, through the long sea journey to India and Africa and finally England, Capek and Machakek had been friends. When a man speaks only the small words of a language that is not his own he finds it hard to express the half-tones of friendship and relief and suffering and most of what Capek and Machakek had suffered together was in Capek's white hair. But now something had happened which was not expressed there but which lay in the dark, wild eyes behind the glasses and the long silences of Capek as he sat staring at the Hurricanes in the sun. His friend Machakek was dead.

The handling of night-fighters is not easy. It was perhaps hard for Capek and Machakek that they should come out of the darkness of Czechoslovakia, through the darkness of the concentration camp and the mine, in order to fight in darkness. It was hard for Machakek who, overshooting the 'drome, hit a telegraph post and died before Capek could get there. It was harder still for Capek, who was now alone.

But the hardest part of it all, perhaps, is that Capek cannot talk to us. He does not know words that will express what he feels about the end of Machakek's journey. He does not know words like endurance and determination, imperishable and undefeated, sacrifice and honour. They are the words, anyway, that are never mentioned at dispersals. He does not know the words for grief and friendship, homesickness and loss. They are never mentioned either. Above all he does not know the words for himself and what he has done.

I do not know the words for Capek either. Looking at his white hair, his dark eyes and his long hands, I am silent now.

Looking Ahead

GRAVEMENT ENDOMMAGÉ

Elizabeth Taylor (1912–1975)

Taylor was a prolific writer who published a total of twelve novels and four collections of short stories. The final year of the war saw the publication of her first novel, *At Mrs Lippincote's* (1945), but she had already been writing and publishing short stories through the 1930s and early 1940s. 'Gravement Endommagé' shows the immediate aftermath of war, a time in which not only buildings and infrastructure but personal relationships needed re-building.

T HE CAR DEVOURED THE ROAD, BUT THE LINES OF POPLARS were without end. The shadows of sagging telegraph wires scalloped the middle of the road, the vaguer shadows of the pretty telegraph posts pleased Louise. They were essentially French, she thought—like, perhaps, lilies of the valley: spare, neatly budded.

The poplars dwindled at intervals and gave place to ruined buildings and pock-marked walls; a landscape of broken stone, faded Dubonnet advertisements. Afterwards, the trees began again.

When they came to a town, the cobblestones, laid fan-wise, slowed up the driving. Outside cafés, the chairs were all empty. Plane trees in the squares half hid the flaking walls of houses with crooked jalousies and frail balconies, like twisted birdcages. All had slipped, subsided.

'But it is so *dead!*' Louise complained, wanting to get to Paris, to take out from her cases her crumpled frocks, shake them out, hang them up. She dreamed of that; she had clung to the idea across the Channel. Because she was sick before the boat moved, Richard thought she was sick deliberately, as a form of revenge. But seasickness ran in her family. Her mother had always been prostrated immediately—as soon (as she so often had said) as her foot touched the deck. It would have seemed an insult to her mother's memory for Louise not to have worked herself up into a queasy panic at the very beginning. Richard, seeing walls sliding past portholes and then sky, finished his drink quickly and went up on deck. Hardier women than Louise leaned over the rails, their scarves flapping, watching the coast of France come up. The strong air had made him hungry, but when they had driven away from the harbour and had stopped for luncheon, Louise would only sip brandy, looking away from his plate.

'But we can never get to Paris by dinner-time,' he said, when they were in the car again. 'Especially driving on the wrong side of the road all the way.'

'There is nowhere between here and there,' she said with authority. 'And I want to *settle*.'

He knew her 'settling'. Photographs of the children spread about, champagne sent up, maids running down corridors with her frocks on their arms, powder spilt everywhere, the bathroom full of bottles and jars. He would have to sit down to telephone a list of names. Her friends would come in for drinks. They would have done better, so far as he could see, to have stayed in London.

'But if we are pushed for time... Why kill ourselves?... After all, this is a holiday... I do remember... There is a place

I stayed at that time… When I first knew you…' Only parts of what he said reached her. The rest was blown away.

'You are deliberately going slow,' she said.

'I think more of my car than to drive it fast along these roads.'

'You think more of your car than of your wife.'

He had no answer. He could not say that at least his car never betrayed him, let him down, embarrassed him, because it constantly did and might at any moment.

'You planned this delay without consulting me. You planned to spend this night in some God-forsaken place and sink into your private nostalgia while my frocks crease and crease…' Her voice mounted up like a wave, trembled, broke.

The holiday was really to set things to rights between them. Lately, trivial bickering had hardened into direct animosity. Relatives put this down to, on his part, overwork, and, on hers, fatigue from the war, during which she had lived, after their London house was bombed, in a remote village with the children. She had nothing to say of those years but that they were not funny. She clung to the children and they to her. He was not, as he said—at first indulgently but more lately with irritation—in the picture. She knit them closer and closer to her, and he was quite excluded. He tried to understand that there must be, after the war, much that was new in her, after so long a gap, one that she would not fill up for him, or discuss. A new quirk was her preoccupation with fashion. To her, it was a race in which she must be first, so she looked *outré* always, never normal. If any of her friends struck a new note before her, she by-passed and cancelled out that particular foible. Men never liked her clothes, and women only admired them. She did not dress for men. Years of almost exclusively feminine society had set up cold antagonisms. Yes, hardship had made her superficial, icily frivolous. For one thing, she now must never be alone. She drank too much. In the night, he knew, she turned and turned, sighing in her sleep, dreaming bad dreams, wherein she could no longer choose her company. When he made love to her, she recoiled in astonishment, as if she could not believe such things could happen.

He had once thought she would be so happy to leave the village, that by comparison her life in London after the war would seem wonderful. But boredom had made her carping, fidgety. Instead of being thankful for what she had, she complained at the slightest discomfort. She raised her standards above what they had ever been; drove maids, who needed little driving, to give notice; was harried, piteous, unrelaxed. Although she was known as a wonderful hostess, guests wonderfully enjoying themselves felt—they could not say why—wary, and listened, as if for a creaking of ice beneath their gaiety.

Her doctor, advising the holiday, was only conventional in his optimism. If anyone were benefited by it, it would be the children, stopping at home with their grandmother— for a while, out of the arena. What Richard needed was a holiday away from Louise, and what Louise needed was a holiday from herself, from the very thing she must always take along, the dull carapace of her own dissatisfaction, her chronic unsunniness.

The drive seemed endless, because it was so monotonous. War had exhaled a vapour of despair over all the scene. Grass grew over grief, trying to hide collapse, to cover some of the wounds. One generation hoped to contend with the failure of another.

Late in the afternoon, they came to a town he remembered. The small cathedral stood like torn lacework against the sky. Birds settled in rows on the empty windows. Nettles grew in the aisle, and stone figures, impaled on rusty spikes of wire, were crumbling away.

But it looks too old a piece of wreckage, he thought. That must be the war before last. Two generations, ruined, lay side by side. Among them, people went on bicycles, to and fro, between the impoverished shops and scarred dwellings.

'After wars, when there is so little time for patching up before the next explosion, what hope is there?' he began.

She didn't answer, stared out of the window, the car jolting so that her teeth chattered.

When Richard was alone in the hotel bedroom, he tried, by spreading about some of Louise's belongings, to make the place seem less temporary. He felt guilty at having had his own way, at keeping her from Paris until the next day and delaying her in this dismal place. It was destined to be, so far as they were concerned, one of those provincial backgrounds, fleeting, meaningless, that travellers erase from experience—the different hotel rooms run together to form one room, this room, any room.

When he had put the pink jars and bottles out in a row above the hand basin, he became dubious. She would perhaps sweep them all back into her case, saying, 'Why unpack before we reach Paris?' and he would find that he had worsened the situation, after all, as he so often did, meaning to better it.

His one piece of selfishness—this halt on the way—she had stubbornly resisted, and now she had gone off to buy picture-postcards for the children, as if no one would think of them if she did not.

Because he often wondered how she looked when he was not there, if her face ever smoothed, he went to the window, hoping to see her coming down the little street. He wanted to catch in advance, to be prepared for, her mood. But she was not moody nowadays. A dreadful consistency discoloured her behaviour.

He pulled the shutters apart and was faced with a waste of fallen masonry, worse now that it was seen from above, and unrecognizable. The humped-up, dark cathedral stood in an untidy space, as if the little shops and cafés he remembered had receded in awe. Dust flowed along the streets, spilling from ruined walls across pavements. Rusty grasses covered debris and everywhere the air was unclean with grit.

Dust, he thought, leaning on the iron rail above window-boxes full of shepherd's-purse—dust has the connotation of despair. In the end, shall we go up in a great swirl of it? He imagined something like the moon's surface, pock-marked, cratered, dry, deserted. When he was young, he had not despaired. Then, autumn leaves, not dust, had blown about these streets; chimes dropped like water, uneven, inconsequential, over rooftops; and the lime-trees yellowed along neat boulevards. Yet, in the entrancement of nostalgia, he remembered, at best, an imperfect happiness and, for the most part, an agony of conjecture and expectancy. Crossing the vestibule of this very hotel, he had turned; his eyes had always sought the letter-rack. The Channel lay between him and his love, who with her timid smile, her mild grimace, had moaned that she could not put pen to paper, was illiterate, never had news; though loving him inordinately, could not spell, never had postage stamps; her ink dried as it approached the page; her parents interrupted. Yes, she had loved him to excess but had seldom written, and now went off in the dust and squalor for picture-postcards for their children.

At the window, waiting for her to appear, he felt that the dust and destruction had pinned down his courage. Day after day had left its residue, sifting down through him—cynicism and despair. He wondered what damage he had wreaked upon her.

Across the street, which once had been narrow and now was open to the sky, a nun went slowly, carrying bread under her arm. The wind plucked her veil. A thin cat followed her. They picked their way across the rubble. The cat stopped once and lifted a paw, licked it carefully, and put it back into the grit. The faint sound of trowel on stone rang out, desultory, hopeless, a frail weapon against so convincing a destruction. That piteous tap, tap turned him away from the window. He could not bear the futility of the sound, or the thought of the monstrous task ahead, and now feared, more than all he could imagine, the sight of his wife hurrying back down the street, frowning, the picture-postcards in her hand.

Louise was late. Richard sat drinking Pernod at a table in the bar where he could see her come into the hotel. There was only the barman to talk to. Rather clouded with drink, Richard leaned on his elbow, describing the town as it had been. The barman, who was Australian, knew only too well. After the '14–'18 war, he had put his savings into a small café across the road. 'I knew it,' Richard said eagerly, forgetting the lacuna in both years and buildings, the gap over which the nun, the cat had picked their way.

'I'll get the compensation some day,' the Australian said, wiping the bar. 'Start again. Something different.'

When a waiter came for drinks, the barman spoke in slow but confident French, probably different from an Englishman's French, Richard thought, though he could not be sure; a Frenchman would know.

'She gets later and later,' he said solemnly.

'Well, if she doesn't come, that's what she's bound to do,' the barman agreed.

'It was a shock to me, the damage of this town.'

'Twelve months ago, you ought to have seen it,' the barman said.

'That's the human characteristic—patience, building up.'

'You might say the same of ants.'

'Making something from nothing,' Richard said. 'I'll take another Pernod.'

The ringing sound of the trowel was in his ears. He saw plodding humanity piling up the bricks again, hanging sacking over the empty windows, temporizing, camping-out in the shadow of even greater disaster, raking ashes, the vision lost. He felt terribly sorry for humanity, as if he did not belong to it. The Pernod shifted him away and made him solitary. Then he thought of Louise and that he must go to look for her. Sometimes she punished him by staying away unaccountably, but knowing that did not lessen his anxiety. He wished that they were at peace together, that the war between them might be over for ever, for if he did not have her, he did not have all he had yearned for; steadied himself with, fighting in the jungle; holding fast, for her, to life; disavowing (with terrible concentration) any danger to her.

He wondered, watching the barman's placid polishing of another man's glasses, if they could begin again, he and Louise, with nothing, from scratch, abandoning the past.

'First I must find her,' he thought. His drinking would

double her fury if she had been lingering to punish him, punishing herself with enforced idling in those unfestive streets; a little scared, he imagined; hesitantly casual.

She came as he was putting a foot unsteadily to the floor. She stood at the door with an unexpectant look. When he smiled and greeted her, she tried to give two different smiles at once—one for the barman to see (controlled, marital), the other less a smile than a negation of it ('I see nothing to smile about').

'Darling, what will you have?'

She surveyed the row of bottles hesitantly, but her hesitation was for the barman's benefit. Richard knew her pause meant an unwillingness to drink in such company, in such a mood, and that in a minute she would say 'A dry Martini,' because once he had told her she should not drink gin abroad. She sat down beside him in silence.

'A nice dry Martini?' he suddenly asked, thinking of the man with the trowel, the nun with the bread, the battered cathedral, everybody's poor start. Again she tried to convey two meanings; to the barman that she was casual about her Martini, to her husband that she was casual about him.

Richard's head was swimming. He patted his wife's knee.

'Did you get the postcards all right?'

'Of course.' Her glance brushed his hand off her knee. 'Cheers!' she held her glass at half-mast very briefly, spoke in the most annulling way, drank. Those deep lines from her nose to her mouth met the glass.

'Cheers, my darling!' he said, watching her. Her annoyance froze the silence.

Oh, from the most unpromising material, he thought, but he did seem to see some glimmer ahead, if only of his own patience, his own perseverance, which appeared, in this frame of mind, in this place, a small demand upon him.

ACCORDING TO THE DIRECTIVE

Inez Holden (1903–1974)

Born into a wealthy and eccentric family, Holden was a novelist, journalist and short story writer. She mixed with bohemian and literary circles and was friends with George Orwell and the poet Stevie Smith, as well as a one-time lodger of H. G. Wells's. She wrote articles and fiction for publications as varied as the *Daily Express*, the *Evening Standard* and the *Manchester Guardian*. During the Second World War, Holden worked in an aircraft factory and was one of the contributors to Cyril Connolly's new literary magazine *Horizon*. 'According to the Directive' captures the mood of the end of the war: victory mingled with despondency, as the war had disrupted millions of lives and torn apart families across Europe and beyond.

T HE DAY THE INFORMATION OFFICER BROUGHT A JOUR-
nalist to the camp a lorry was waiting in the yard to take
some of the Displaced Persons away.

Those who were leaving stood shoulder to shoulder in
the back of the lorry clasping the packets of chocolates and
cigarettes which they had been given for the journey. Some
of them also carried bunches of flowers which they held, like
Victorian posies, closely to their chests.

Some wooden steps had been placed against the back of
the lorry. The last man to walk wearily upwards wore a long
grey overcoat, a peaked cap and dark blue civilian trousers; he
carried a cheap cardboard suitcase and he smiled as the others
moved to make room for him beside them.

A man in uniform stood by with a list; when the last
Displaced Person had answered, and had his name checked
against the list, the steps were taken away. A little group waited
in the yard to wave goodbye to their friends as they drove out
of the camp.

Lisa Wilson asked where the people were going. 'Are they
all on the way home?' she said.

'On the way home,' Edward Syler repeated. 'No, I don't think so. The lorry's on the way to Hanover, maybe there's a convoy going from there and perhaps a few will be repatriated, but I reckon the majority are just planning to link up with friends in other camps. No doubt they've all got permission to visit relatives in some distant DP Assembly Centre, but of course you can't believe everything they say.'

'No, I suppose not.'

Edward Syler, the Information Officer, wore pince-nez but they were strong pince-nez, bridged together with a tough piece of metal. His shirt had been washed so often and so earnestly that it had lost its original khaki and become almost cream coloured; he wore a faded field-jacket and he had a shouting manner as if he was forever lecturing to a group of deaf foreigners.

'Well now, Miss Wilson, you've come here to write a feature on DPs,' he said. 'So you just go ahead and ask me any questions you like.'

'What about the last man in the lorry,' Lisa said. 'Wasn't that a Wehrmacht coat he was wearing?'

'Yes, I guess so. As I told you I used to be in this camp myself as a Welfare Officer. That Italian guy was already here when I arrived, I remember he had some story about being forced into the German Army—anyhow, he went on wearing his Wehrmacht overcoat on cold days because he didn't have any other coat—of course he must have been an ex-enemy alien when he first came into the camp and according to the directive he wouldn't have been entitled to DP status—we used to get all sorts here you know, Poles, Balts, Turks and one or two types claiming British or American citizenship. Why, we even had Mennonites.'

'Mennonites, what are they?'

'Oh, they're an agricultural community, they mostly came from Russia, they'd been driven right across two continents and finally landed up here. They don't believe in war.'

'How do you mean they don't believe in war? They must have noticed that something of the sort was going on around them.'

'Oh, sure, they noticed that there was some shooting, many of them were killed, but they don't take an active part in war themselves. Their religion forbids it.'

As Syler and Lisa walked slowly across the courtyard Syler said, 'I thought we'd go across to the Sick Bay, you might get a story there.' He rattled through some statistics and then he said, 'Well, I reckon you're familiar with the overall DP situation in Germany right now.'

Lisa wondered where Syler came from. 'Are you an American?' she asked him.

'An American? Hell no,' he said. 'I was born in Tokyo and educated in Heidelberg, but both my parents were of British nationality, though I've spent a number of years in the United States. My second wife came from Florida. I've never regretted marrying an American.'

'Is your wife in Europe now?'

'I dunno,' Syler said. 'We were divorced some while back. Well, here's the Camp Sick Bay, but of course there are only convalescents here. We have a directive to send all serious cases straight to the hospital in the town.'

There were sixteen beds in the Sick Bay but only four of them were occupied. One man was sitting on the edge of his bed, he wore a check shirt and grey flannel trousers. His black hair was parted in the middle, his eyes were dark with a melancholy expression, but he smiled all the time as if to show that he knew, more than anyone else, what was going on around him.

'Another Italian?' Lisa asked.

'No, a Frenchman,' Syler said.

At the far end of the room a man with a blackened face and close-cropped hair leant back against the coarse cotton of his pillow reading in a low tone from a book which he held in both hands as if afraid that someone might try to take it from him. He did not look up as Edward and Lisa came in but continued to read, his lips moving rapidly and his eyes, which were red-rimmed and distressingly bloodshot, staying open all the time.

On the other side of the room a fair-haired boy, propped up by two pillows, lay back with both his eyes closed.

Near the entrance, and opposite the check-shirted Frenchman, an old man, with frail transparent hands and a long thin face, was sitting up in bed. Edward Syler walked over to him.

'Well, Monsieur Dumaine,' Syler said. 'How are you getting on?'

Dumaine inclined his head graciously and answered in French. He said that he was not getting the right diet. 'Some of the food I eat now is not at all good for me in my enfeebled state.'

The check-shirted convalescent on the bed opposite gave a contemptuous smile.

The old man went into elaborate explanations of the kind of diet which, he believed, would suit him best. 'Diet,' he said, 'is a very subtle and important thing. We live by what we eat, and, in fact, it affects all our thoughts. But I shall recover quickly when I have all I need. On Monday I take the train to Paris.'

'But it is not certain that you will be able to go to France,' Syler told him.

'Why not?' Dumaine asked sharply.

Syler looked round the room as if seeking some help from the convalescents, but the man with the blackened face still muttered on at the same speed and in the same tone, the fair-haired boy kept his eyes closed and the man in the check shirt did not give up his sneering smile.

'Well, Monsieur Dumaine,' Syler said. 'You had better see the French liaison officer, he will explain all the circumstances.'

'Circumstances,' Dumaine said. 'I have no need to be told anything about them. I know my own circumstances only too well—who better?' But after these words the old man's thoughts seemed to wander away from the camp and the convalescents' room. He began to talk about his farm in France. 'We had plenty of cheese there,' he said. 'Cheese and butter,' and with one thin hand he made a swirling movement round and round as if he was churning butter in a bowl. 'And when I am there again I shall make more cheese and butter and look after animals and so become a farmer as before.'

The check-shirted convalescent on the bed opposite laughed softly.

The fair-haired boy had opened his eyes and he was leaning on his elbow staring. Syler walked over to him. 'Well, Harry,' he said. 'How's the rheumatism?'

'It's better, thank you,' the boy answered. 'But I sleep a lot.'

'Ah, that's what you want,' Syler said in his shouting manner. 'Plenty of rest and you'll soon be all right. Now here is Miss Wilson, a journalist from London, to see you.'

'I'm from London, too,' said the boy. 'I was born there in Castle Street.' He was silent for a few moments nervously touching the covers of a book lying on the bed.

'What have you been reading there?' Syler asked.

'World history,' the boy told him. 'But in the Red Cross Club last month I was reading an illustrated paper. There were some pictures of cadets training. It shows that they do accept boys of my age as soldiers. I should like to join the British Army now.'

'He's been reading about Sandhurst,' Syler explained. 'It's true, isn't it, Harry, that you walked here all the way from Danzig?'

'From Danzig. Yes.'

'Without food or water?'

'No,' the boy said. 'I had some water to drink on the way.'

'How many days did it take?'

'It took ten days,' Harry answered.

'A long journey.'

'Yes, it was a long journey.'

The camp doctor came in. The check-shirted man stood up. Dumaine, looking forward to further conversations about his diet, waved his hand in greeting, but the man with the blackened face went on reading aloud.

'Come on,' Syler said. 'Let's get out of here.'

As they walked across the courtyard Syler said, 'I keep asking them questions. Maybe you can pick up a story from some of their talk.'

'Yes,' Lisa said. 'Maybe I can. Will the boy Harry be able to go back to England soon?'

'No, I don't think so. You see,' Syler said, 'his father was killed in the Wehrmacht, his mother died during an air raid on Hamburg, the boy says he was born in Castle Street, London, but there's no trace of him in that district at all. The British haven't accepted him for citizenship, he has no relatives, no friends, no proof of how his early life was spent, so he must wait in the camp till all these questions have been cleared up.'

'How old is he?'

'It is believed that he has just passed his fourteenth birthday.'

'Oh, I see. Too young to decide his own future.'

'It's not so much a question of age as of nationality. You see, he's the son of a German father, and, as far as we know, of a German mother, he speaks perfect English and he wants to be British, but that doesn't make him British. If there was no definite ruling on this sort of thing we'd be snowed under with Germans claiming to be British. You'd be surprised how many Germans want to be British, nowadays.'

'I daresay. What about Dumaine? He seems to think he'll be going back to France on Monday.'

'Yes, he thinks so, but he won't be going. You see, according to an USFET* directive, all western nationals must return to their homes before the fifteenth of this month. That's next Monday. Their alternative is to join the German economy with its certainty of lower rations and likelihood of unemployment.'

'It sounds harsh.'

'Yeah, but it isn't. It only applies to a few hundred DPs, French, Dutch, Belgians and so on. They can't have any reason for staying here unless they've been collaborators.'

'Then why can't Dumaine go back?'

'Because he's a collaborator. In any case there's some uncertainty about his nationality, it's being investigated right now. He speaks French and German equally well. Mostly he speaks a mixture of both. He may be German. Of course it's true what he says about his farm in France. But I don't suppose he'll ever see it again.'

---

* United States Forces European Theatre.

'But surely a feeble old man of eighty years old wouldn't be likely to start a Fascist revival wherever he went?'

'No, but you see Dumaine's war work rules him right out. He was employed by the Todt Organization. He's quite frank about it himself, he says, "I needed a job so I offered my services to the Germans as an interpreter." Well, the Todt Organization was a Nazi set-up, so Dumaine couldn't be accepted in France now.'

'No, I see that. What will happen to him?'

'If it's proved that he's a German he will be moved to the German refugee hospital about a quarter of a mile from here. Wherever Dumaine goes he'll be the hell of a nuisance. I remember when he came into the camp. He refused, at first, to go through the usual de-lousing process and he wanted a room of his own and all that sort of thing.'

The winter was over and the sun was shining through the black boughs of three slender trees which had survived the bombardment, grass was already struggling up through the uneven ground giving the edge of the courtyard a green and hopeful look.

'Well, what do you think of the DP Camp?' Syler said. 'Can you get a story out of it?'

'I don't know yet,' Lisa answered. 'I was still thinking about the convalescents' room. What about the man in the end bed?'

'Oh, you mean the Bible reader? No one knows who he is. He arrived in the camp with a completely burnt and blackened face and red-rimmed eyes. He still looks the same way, but he was much worse then. He had a brown paper parcel with him

and he could only say, "I was in the centre of an explosion."
He said it over and over again, in perfect Polish without any
accent. The brown paper parcel contained some clean under-
clothes and a Bible in German—nothing else. So that guy just
lies there all day reading the holy scriptures in German, but
we think he may be Polish.'

'Will he be sent back to Poland then?'

'Well, according to the directive nationals can return to
the country of their origin but we don't know anything of
this man's origin—neither does he. A Pole must prove he's
a Pole before he can go to Poland. We haven't been able to
find anyone who knows the Bible reader and it's doubtful if
they could recognize him the way he is now, and of course
we can't expect any help from him, his memory's gone. He
is, in fact, now mad.'

'He's a bit beyond the reach of directives then?'

Syler seemed to feel affronted, as if he were a man of
honour whose sister had just been insulted in public. 'Nothing's
beyond the reach of directives,' he said. 'The directives are OK.
They've all been planned on a high level.'

As they made their way towards the Assembly Room they
passed a long wooden corridor which connected the sick bay
with the main building. The corridor had been divided into
a series of small offices and in the centre there was a larger
room with wide windows.

'See that room?' Syler said. 'I was responsible for that when
I was here. I had it made into a little library.'

There were only two people in the wide-windowed room, a young man wearing a Norfolk jacket, and the boots and breeches of the continental refugee, and a girl with long straight hair who held a book in her hand but did not appear to be reading.

'Of course, there's nobody much there now,' Syler said. 'The rest are working outside, or in the administration of the camp, but that little library has been a big success. The DP Committee said it was a grand idea. I fixed for the bookshelves to be six foot along the back and eight foot four along the side walls. We painted them white.'

'Who's the girl in there?' Lisa asked.

'The girl? Oh, she's Polish, she used to belong to a large family. She told me how they all used to go to a country house each summer—all the aunts, uncles, nephews, nieces, cousins and grandparents—they were thirty-seven in all. What d'you know about that? Thirty-seven in one family. But now none are left—all killed or lost, deported by the Russians, killed in air raids or in the Warsaw Rising. 'Course the majority were murdered by the SS. The girl and her sister were liberated from Auschwitz by the Allies but the sister committed suicide a few weeks later. This girl won't go back to Warsaw, she says she'd be willing to go to the United States but there's no one to sponsor her. I guess she'll have to wait for mass emigration.'

'What about the man—the other DP in there?'

'Oh, he's not a DP, he's an Infiltree. He was in this camp as a DP but he was repatriated to Poland, then he came back here.

Maybe he's holding out for Palestine.' Edward Syler peered into the library room. 'Some of the paint's got scratched,' he said sadly. ''Course we were very short of paint in this camp; and that's how it is that some of the Germans' slogans are still up in the passages. This place used to be one of Ley's Labour Ministries you know.'

When Syler took Lisa into the Assembly Room she saw that there was a frieze round the wall of square-shouldered German workers painted in pastel colours, some with hammers or spanners, some with pick-axes and others with spades.

Lisa stared at the large-limbed lifeless figures. 'A bit depressing, aren't they?'

'Sure they're depressing, but we'd need the hell of a lot of paint to paint them out.'

At the end of the room there was a noticeboard. 'Reminds me of school,' Lisa said.

'Oh, the noticeboard. There's all kinds of notices up there, the concerts the DPs organize for themselves, the elections for the DP Commandant, the classes in the DP school and now this census they're planning to take on how many of those who come from Russian occupied territory are willing to go back there.'

Lisa looked at the notice and saw that someone had scribbled on it in pencil. 'No. Don't want to go back because they take away your food card, and also they hang you.'

Syler stared closely at the noticeboard through his pince-nez. 'They're very confused right now,' he said. 'We may as well leave this camp if we want to get to the other camp in good time. It's mainly a Transit Camp.'

As they walked towards Syler's car Lisa said, 'What about that dark man in the convalescents' room. I mean the Frenchman—is he going back to France on Monday?'

'Oh, yeah. The guy in the check shirt. Sure he's going, but he doesn't want to. He says he served five years in the French navy and he's been in the French police force too, but the authorities in France sent for him—that was during the occupation, of course—there was some doubt about his activities and they informed him that he wasn't a Frenchman—it seems his mother was Italian. When he told me this story he said, "I can stand a good deal, but when they told me I wasn't a Frenchman that was another matter—I didn't hesitate an instant, I thought if they say I'm an Italian all right I'll be an Italian, and I came voluntarily into Germany." Of course none of this was official—off the record you know—don't quote me. As a matter of fact I wasn't very clear about what had happened to him and nothing he told me made much sense.'

'It looks as if he was as much a collaborator as Dumaine.'

'Oh, no, he comes into the category of "forced worker". There's no evidence that he collaborated with the Germans, he's not a political type at all. He belongs to the criminal class really. You can't believe much he says, he's an experienced liar and very bitter because his nationality was called into question.'

As they entered the yard two men were coming back into the camp from work in the fields, they both wore military mackintosh capes which did not fit them very well and gave them a comic air.

'See those two men?' Syler said.

'Yes.'

'Mennonites. Don't believe in war. See?'

When they had been driving for a little while and the camp was out of sight Syler stopped the car and said that he had two bottles of cognac with him. 'Wouldn't go on a trip without liquor,' he said. 'I've brought a glass for you.' He opened the bottle and poured some out for Lisa, but he himself drank out of the bottle, throwing his head back as if he was a GI drinking Coca-Cola.

'The mortality rate amongst the Anglo-American personnel in Berlin is very high just now,' he said.

'What do they die of?'

'Oh, "mortality rate"—that's just a figure of speech. I mean the guys that get sent home with DTs.'

After Syler had drunk some more he began to talk, in a soft voice, about a woman he was planning to meet in Berlin. 'You ought to meet my girlfriend,' he said. 'You'd like her, you know, she's sympathetic, that's what she is, sympathetic. To tell you the truth, I aim to marry her.'

'Another American?' Lisa asked.

'No, she's German. Most of her relatives are interned or something, so she's all alone now. She hasn't got anyone but me.' Syler sighed deeply. 'Still, she'll be all right when we're married.'

'Have you got permission already?' Lisa asked.

'Permission?'

'Yes, you do have to get permission before you can marry a German national, don't you? I mean the official consent of your superior officer, according to the directive.'

Syler stared at the bottle of cognac as if it was an enemy. Then he shouted, 'Aw, to hell with the directive. What do I care about directives?' He started up the car, and, peering through his pince-nez at the long white road before him, he drove on in silence to the Transit Camp.